TO

G

W

ROSA GOLUB

ASSTHER

novum ✺ premium

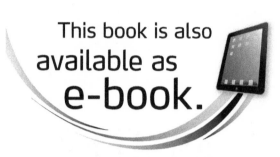

This book is also
available as
e-book.

www.novumpublishing.com

© 2021 novum publishing

ISBN 978-1-64268-132-1
Editing: Karen Simmering
Cover photos: Alina Prochan,
Yufa12379 | Dreamstime.com
Cover design, layout & typesetting:
novum publishing

www.novumpublishing.com

To my family.
Thank you for all your love and support.

PART I

Chapter 1

1

Assther pushed her sluggish eyelids open and blinked several times, then turned her head to each side. Groggy and disoriented, she tasted metal. Almost immediately, her senses were absorbing the surroundings and transmitting the information to her brain for analysis. It would take some time to collect and organize the onslaught of data her brain was receiving. However, Assther was hammered by a barrage of questions and was caught in an endless loop of fear and despair. It was imperative, she realized, to control her racing thoughts and direct her mind to the critical situation at hand.

"Where am I? Why am I here?" Assther asked in a hoarse voice; her throat was parched. "What are you going to do to me?" she added, her voice trembling. Something approached Assther and regarded her with its enormous eyes for several minutes. Then it blinked several times and silently joined its colleagues on the other side of the room.

Glancing around, Assther saw beings wearing red suits moving from station to station. Each of them had a large hump on its back, and they seemed to glide over the polished floor. Numerous beds with motionless figures were situated around the egg-shaped room. Oblong bulbs glowing alternatively yellow and green illuminated the space. The bioluminescent lights cast a soothing glow over the room. The scent of lavender and chamomile permeated the room, and the intensity ebbed and flowed.

Scanning the room, Assther located a silver canister affixed to the clay wall from which a fine mist hissed out at regular intervals. In addition, she noticed compound eye-shaped orbs throughout the room. She was being watched.

Assther turned to inspect her own condition. She was blanketed with a transparent gelatinous cushion and attached to sensors monitoring her vitals: blood pressure, heart rate, respiration, and others she couldn't decipher. These devices were different than any monitors she'd d ever seen; the displays were more sophisticated and emitted a low melodious chime, which comforted her. *Where exactly am I? Who are these entities who have this type of technology?* she wondered.

Black tubes were inserted on either side of her, and Assther discovered that she was naked. Despite seeing no restraints, she was unable to move freely. Assther's anxiety increased as she struggled against them and the pipes hindered her movements. *Why am I naked? What are the tubes for?* she thought in despair.

Where is my father? What had happened to him? Is he safe? What will my future be with these beings? Her emotions were in turmoil. Assther's concern for her father's safety and alarm about her own well-being were increasing by the minute.

Initially, Assther feared that something bad had happened to her father, but this idea was instantly dismissed; she was unable to process it. Every nerve in Assther's body was ablaze. Surely these creatures wouldn't have brought her here to cause her harm, she reasoned.

Where's Suzie? Assther thought with a sudden flash. Her heart was choked with concern and despair. Forcing her mind to retrieve her last memories, Assther remembered she'd visited her father at his house, and they were discussing something important. Her father's face had been haggard and worn as he explained the situation to Assther. She'd listened silently, absorbing all the facts. After her father had finished, the two of them had decided on a course of action. *Why didn't he keep his promise?*

Meanwhile, several feet away and in another room, Assther's father was restrained on a similar bed, attached to similar sensors, monitored by similar beings, and undergoing a similar evaluation. Unfortunately, Assther was unaware of it.

The din of blaring alarms wrenched Assther back to reality. A creature unfurled its gossamer wings and darted to her bedside. Assther turned just in time to see the being fold them behind its back. A black-gloved extremity reached out, and the digits danced across the screen in front of it.

"Could you please cover me?" Assther asked, scrutinizing the beings closely.

"No need," replied the being as it adjusted the monitor to address Assther's agitated state. It was completely masked, and Assther could only see its humanoid eyes. The creature was slender and bony, and Assther sensed a low musical hum emanating from it whenever it approached her. The sound rose and fell in intensity like a string quartet.

"Please cover me up."

The creatures continued with their tasks, busying themselves around the room. Finally, one stopped, turned, and asked, "Are you cold?" Without waiting for her reply, it darted away.

Of course the gelatinous mat must be keeping me warm, Assther thought, *but why don't they understand why I want to be covered?*

Out of the corner of her eye, Assther saw a group of them moving toward her and felt her stomach tighten. *What's going on? What are they going to do to me now?* She began struggling for air. One of them, observing the change on the monitor, increased the volume of the chimes. Soon, Assther felt a wave of euphoria, and as she struggled against drowsiness, she heard a voice say, "Time to access her memories."

Chapter 2

1

The day Assther's mother was buried was a typical Bay Area winter day. A thick fog enveloped the city, and intermittent drizzle and heavy showers were forecasted. The cemetery, which was over a hundred years old, was located on the outskirts of town and was ringed by a metal fence. Many of the weather-beaten tombstones were fragmented, rendering the names of the deceased virtually unreadable. The grassy knolls were soggy and the dirt pathways muddy from the rain that had fallen the previous days.

The group of mourners gathered at the cemetery to honor the life of Hannah Medina, which had ended too soon. They stood close to the gravesite, which had been dug by the gravediggers the night before; the wooden casket would soon have its final resting place.

Shortly after the group begun to say the Mourner's Kaddish,"*Yitgadal v'yitkadash sh'mei raba b'alma di-v'ra-,*" the rain intensified, and a driving wind upended several umbrellas. Most of the mourners raced for cover to their cars, leaving only the immediate family behind. The prayer was finished hastily, and the casket was gently lowered by the cemetery workers.

Assther, her father Carlos, and Hannah's family took turns throwing dirt onto the casket, emblematic of the phrase "dirt to dirt, ashes to ashes." Later, the workers would cover up the grave, and a small marker would remain with the name, Hannah Medina. The following year, Assther and her family would return to the gravesite to commemorate the unveiling of the tombstone.

Standing by the grave using a shovel, Carlos could smell the earth and see the casket where his beloved Hannah's body was encased. As he took his turn scooping the earth into the grave, Carlos observed himself floating over the gathering watching the service. He performed the task mechanically because his mind couldn't accept that he would never see his beloved again.

Hannah's parents were visibly distraught and clinging to each other. His teenage daughter was sobbing softly, her petite frame trembling. Moving closer to her, Carlos wrapped his arms around his daughter and embraced her.

As the rest of crowd dispersed, Carlos remained at the gravesite with Assther. They were both soaked. A light rain continued to fall, and they abandoned the umbrella. Carlos gazed up at the maple tree, now leafless but still magnificent with its extended boughs. The last time he'd seen it, the tree had been full of life, its large canopy of deep green, fan-shaped leaves softly fluttering in the spring air. The insects were gorging on the vibrant and assorted plants on the hillside.

Carlos looked at the barren and lifeless scene, which reflected his own state. In a few months, the tree and surrounding hillside would be transformed by the splendor of spring's metamorphosis. But Carlos knew he would never feel alive again.

Feeling unsteady, Carlos leaned against his daughter for support. *Oh Hannah, I can't believe you're gone!* he thought. After several minutes, Carlos and Assther departed slowly toward the car and drove home. It was time to sit *shiva* for Hannah.

2

As a child, Assther didn't understand the concept of visiting people in mourning. The only other funeral she'd attended was when her great-grandmother Ruth had died in her sleep three years before. Nana Ruth had been independent until the day she was found deceased by her neighbor in her apartment. Her passing was a great shock to the entire family. At the *shiva*, Assther remembered hearing her Aunt Leah say, "At least she went peacefully and didn't suffer."

Driving home after the funeral, Assther remembered people had brought a lot of food when her grandmother passed. In her opinion, they'd stayed too long and talked too much. It would be the same people at her home today and she would have to be the hostess. The last thing Assther wanted to do was entertain people.

Entering her home with apprehension, Assther was relieved that the role of hostess was taken by her Aunt Leah, who was bustling around ensuring everyone had enough food and drinks. As soon as Aunt Leah saw Assther, she rushed toward her and instructed, "Go upstairs and quickly change out of those wet clothes. Then meet me in the kitchen. I need your help." Immediately, Aunt Leah turned on her heels and disappeared into the kitchen.

Terrific! All Assther wanted to do was be in her room by herself. Was that too much to ask for?

After changing her clothes, Assther descended the stairs and walked toward to the kitchen. On her way, she noticed that the mirrors in the house were covered in black cloth. After entering the room, Assther swept her eyes over the scene. The granite counters contained enough food for two banquets. Assther's aunt owned a catering company and had provided the food for the *shiva*. Aunt Leah had a fear of running out of food, and she usually prepared too much.

Perched on a stool near the counter, Aunt Leah sipped her Pinot Noir, holding the wine glass with her right hand. A half-empty bottle sat nearby. Upon seeing Assther enter, she turned her head and her eyes were moist.

"Hello, honey," Aunt Leah said, her voice faltering. "Come here, please." She extended her arm toward Assther. Cautiously, Assther approached.

Aunt Leah lifted her hand and gently stroked Assther's right cheek. "How are you doing, Assther?"

"Okay …I guess," Assther replied.

"Good," Leah said, hanging her head. "That's good." Tears were silently streaming down her face. After exhaling deeply, Leah looked up at Assther and said, "I need you to take the food out there." She paused. "I …I just can't do it right now." Leah buried her face in her hands and wept, her thick shoulders trembling.

Assther embraced her aunt and fought to suppress her own emotions. "Don't worry, Aunt Leah. I'll take care of it." Assther picked up the tray and rushed out of the kitchen into the living room.

While moving around the room offering refreshments to the guests, she was approached by a lanky man with slender fingers.

"Thank you, young lady," he said as he reached for an hors d'oeuvre.

"You're welcome, sir," Assther said, slightly unnerved by the enormous man.

She deliberately avoided the foyer, where an enlarged picture of her mother was being displayed on a stand. A guest sign-in book was placed on a wooden table next to the photo. When she entered the house earlier, Assther had seen both items. In the picture her mother was youthful and vibrant. Assther couldn't reconcile the person staring back at her with the how her mother had changed at the end of her life.

The incessant murmur of the whispering voices grated on her nerves and she couldn't believe the small house could accommodate so many people.

Placing the half-empty tray on the coffee table, Assther went to check on her father.

Carlos had collapsed in the living room in his chair and was staring at the mantle where his wedding picture rested. Looking at the image of his dearest, resplendent in her wedding gown, Carlos' fingers clenched the arm rests. Then his hands began to tremble. Despite hearing the distant chatter of the assembled guests and the clanging of silverware against the china, Carlos didn't register it. When approached by family and friends, Carlos uttered short, one-word replies. Still soaked from the rain, he didn't t feel it. He was immobilized and numb from grief.

Gazing up at the picture of his beloved, Carlos saw her brown eyes looking back at him, and in his mind he spoke with her just as they always had. *What do I do now?* he implored. *How do I survive without you? Don't you know that I was worthless without you? Now I'll return to being worthless once more. How do I care for our daughter without you?* He received no response.

Rising from his chair, Carlos walked to the record player and turned the machine on. He placed an Oscar Peterson album on the turntable and shifted the arm, dropping the needle into the groove. The saxophone solo wailed, and the noises in the house stopped momentarily as the mourners looked at Carlos. Oblivious, Carlos returned to his chair and shut his eyes.

After bringing her father a plate of food, Assther knelt down next to him. Carlos was in his chair with a vacant gaze and an anguished expression on his face.

"Papi," Assther whispered softly, "please eat something."

Mutely, Carlos continued to stare at the picture.

Assther touched his arm softly. "Papi," she said, "I need you to eat for me." Assther kissed her father gently on the cheek and sighed heavily. She was beginning to worry about her father, but she needed to help her aunt.

"I'll check on you in a little bit."

While Assther was clearing the plates and picking up the garbage, she noticed her Aunt Judy sitting on the couch nearby. Aunt Judy's had a tendency to talk loudly and Assther heard parts of the conversation.

"First my dear sister married a *goy*," Assther heard Aunt Judy say. Assther turned in her aunt's direction and saw that her aunt's mascara was smeared, and the makeup looked worse than usual. Aunt Judy was speaking with another woman Assther didn't recognize. Assther moved closer and busied herself with the cleaning, sensing she needed to hear the rest of this conversation.

"Then Hannah couldn't have any kids," Aunt Judy said, dabbing her raccoon eyes with a tissue and leaving stray bits of paper on her face.

Assther had been aware that her mother's family hadn't initially approved of her father. *But they love him now. Right? What's Aunt Judy talking about my mother not being able to have children? She must be wrong!*

"Now this happened," Judy was saying. "It's like the trials of Job!"

Aunt Judy's tears were streaming down her face and her eyes were swollen and red. She blew her nose with a clean tissue.

Assther felt a wave of nausea and a knot forming in her stomach. Unable to listen any longer, Assther grabbed the soiled dishes and rushed into the kitchen. She slammed the dishes on the counter, almost breaking her parents' wedding china.

What's that old lady talking about? Assther thought, alarmed and angry. Assther's tears felt hot against her face as she dashed up the stairs to her room and slammed the door shut.

3

As sunset approached, it was time to go to Temple to recite the Mourner's Kaddish for Assther's mother. The prayer was a vital component of the mourning process, and Assther knew it was important to her father and would've been important to her mother as well.

"Assther, please open the door," Carlos said, gently knocking. "Mija," he said, "we need to go to Temple. Please open up."

After Assther unbolted the lock, Carlos walked into his teenage daughter's bedroom. Salmon-colored curtains adorned each side of the windows, posters of her favorite bands were affixed on the lavender-colored walls, and various stuffed animals congregated on the pink bedspread. The bookcase was full of books that Carlos and Hannah had read to her at bedtime. On the dresser was the picture of the three of them at the beach. Carlos could still smell the ocean and hear Hannah's laugh as she tried to keep her hat from blowing away.

Holding her favorite brown stuffed bear, Juki, Assther was sitting on her bed rocking back and forth. Her face was wet, and her eyes were red. Silently, Carlos sat next to his daughter and pulled her close to his chest. Before long, they were both weeping.

"I miss her too," he whispered. Carlos sighed heavily, feeling heaviness in his chest. Rhythmically he stroked his child's hair.

4

The heavy double doors of the Temple swung open, and Assther and her father rushed through into the anteroom, which was decorated with large-scale multicolored stained-glass images of the Ten Commandments. They were just in time for the evening prayer services. Rabbi Tesfaye walked toward them at a brisk pace, his long legs moving him quickly along the carpeted floor. His gentle brown eyes locked on both of them, and he extended his olive-toned hand.

"Assther, Carlos, I'm so very sorry about Hannah," Rabbi Tesfaye said. "She was a wonderful soul and we will all miss seeing her." He paused. "This place won't be the same without her. She is truly irreplaceable."

"Rabbi, I want to thank you for everything you did for our family," Carlos said. "It was only after you began working at the Temple that Hannah wanted to attend services. She enjoyed helping the community and felt this place was her home." Carlos swallowed hard.

"I'm very happy to hear that," the rabbi said. "I can assure you, we gained more from her contribution than she realized. Please, it's time for the prayer. We've made a special place for the two of you. Follow me." The rabbi led Carlos and Assther to the sanctuary. After settling in the pews, both retrieved the prayer books and prepared for the service to begin.

Prior to Rabbi Tesfaye's arrival, Hannah had joked about the family being High Holiday Jews. With his arrival, the Medinas had become increasingly more involved in the Temple, which delighted Hannah's parents. Hannah had even convinced Assther to have her Bat Mitzvah on her twelfth birthday.

Gazing up at the *bimah,* Carlos remembered Assther's Bat Mitzvah. On that day, his daughter had recited a Torah portion in front of the congregation. After the rabbi had retrieved the coiled scrolls from the glass case, he had placed it gently on the podium. Draped in a tallit, Assther had gingerly smoothed the parchment with her fingers. Grasping the long pointer, she had begun to read. Carlos remembered Hannah's proud face upon hearing her daughter chant those sacred words. He ached to return to that day.

As the congregation began the prayer services, Assther and Carlos joined in.

Prior to the Mourner's Kaddish, various congregation members uttered the names of the ill or recently deceased, to which Rabbi Tesfaye added Hannah Bat Abraham.

"Yitgadal v'yitkadash sh'mei raba b'alma di-v'ra chirutei, v'yamlich malchutei b'chayeichon ...," the group recited.

To honor Hannah, Assther and her father would return for the next six days.

Chapter 3

1

Several weeks after the funeral, Assther and Carlos ordered pizza for dinner; it had been some time since either one of them had been hungry. After the pizza arrived, Carlos placed the pie on the counter and lifted the lid, preparing to serve it. Immediately, Carlos and Assther stared at the pie and then at each other. Carlos began panting. He fumbled for the chair and collapsed into it.

Observing her father's reaction, Assther quickly closed the pizza cover and slid it across the granite countertop. After retrieving two bowls and a box of corn flakes from the cupboard, Assther poured the cereal into the dishes. Then she pulled the milk from the fridge and placed everything on the kitchen table.

After wiping her hands on a kitchen towel, Assther perched on the chair beside her father. "It's okay, Papi," she reassured him, placing an arm on his back. "We don't have to have the pizza. Let's just have some cereal."

For several minutes, Carlos regarded his daughter mutely.

"That was your mother's favorite topping. How could I have ordered her favorite pizza?"

"It's just pizza. It'll be okay," Assther said, embracing him.

But Assther knew it was much more than just pizza.

2

For the next few weeks, Assther and Carlos attempted to eat dinner regularly, which were mostly halfhearted efforts. For some time, Assther had intended to ask her father about Aunt Judy's comment. She'd been replaying the remark repeatedly, obsessively, in her mind. However, Assther didn't want to hurt him in his already fragile state. And, she was worried about his reaction. Yet, she was tormented by the comments. *What did Aunt Judy mean when she said my mother was unable to have children? Did it mean I was adopted? Who is my real mother, then? Is Carlos my real father?* These questions distressed her as her mind invented various scenarios, and the disturbing possibilities fueled her insomnia.

Several weeks later, Assther looked over at her father while they were sitting down for lunch together at the local beanery. He looked more pensive than usual, and Assther became concerned. The diner was crowded, and Assther had to speak above the noise to be heard.

"What's wrong, Papi?" she asked. *Please don't tell me you're sick too!* Assther watched her father absentmindedly scrape the grease from the edge of the table. Then Carlos folded his menu and took a sip of water.

"Nothing, mija. It's just time for you to go back to school," Carlos said with a sigh. His hands were fidgeting in front of him.

"It's been several weeks since you were in school," her father said. "I think it's time for you to restart. What do you think?"

"I don't know," Assther said in a subdued voice. "Whatever you think is best."

Assther and Carlos glanced up as a waiter stood in front of them. His soiled apron touched the table, and he breathed audibly though his bulbous nose.

"You two know what you—?" A loud noise distracted him, and he added, "Excuse me for a second."

The couple in the next booth were arguing, and their voices were heard over the racket of the other patrons. Assther and Carlos watched the waiter's large body move surprisingly swiftly to the other booth. The waiter's coarse wheezing became more pronounced as the diner suddenly turned quiet.

"If you two can't keep your voices down," the waiter said, looking at each member of the group, "I'm afraid you'll need to leave."

Carlos shook his head, closed his eyes, and massaged his temples. Then he cleared his throat and grasped Assther's hand. "We both need to cope with our grief and move forward with our lives," he said, swallowing hard.

19

"Okay," Assther said. But she sensed there was another matter he wanted to discuss with her. Assther studied her father's grave face. Then she watched Carlos retrieve an envelope from his pocket and hand her a letter.

"What's this?" Assther asked, examining what she had been given.

"Mom wrote you a letter before she died and asked me" – he paused to catch his breath and regain his composure – "to give it to you."

The envelope was pink and on it was written 'To Assther.' Assther felt her heart become taut as she drew the letter close to her chest. A current of raw emotion was rising within her. At that moment, Assther realized how much she longed to see her mother once more, how much she wished to touch her and hear her voice again. Assther felt a knot forming in her stomach and was unsure whether she was ready to read her mother's words.

What had her mother written in the letter? Would it provide any answers to the questions that had been consuming her? Assther decided this wasn't the appropriate time to broach the subject with her father.

3

Another sun had descended on a day without his beloved, and Carlos felt the anguish of his loss just as acutely as the day he'd lost her. Sighing deeply, he raked his fingers through his wild hair as he turned the pink envelope around in his hand. Sitting in his chair, Carlos studied their wedding picture, holding the letter Hannah had written him. He'd finally steeled himself to read it – or at least to start to read it.

The letter read: 'To Ricky, with all my love.' Carlos fingered the writing as a tear streamed down his brown face. He opened the letter gingerly, trying not to damage it. Unfolding the pages slowly, Carlos wanted to feel his beloved in the words, the ink, and the paper. Dried tears stained the letter, which began with Hannah's handwriting, but someone else had finished it.

Carlos could hardly catch his breath. *Oh God*, he thought. *She must've been in too much pain to write the entire letter and needed help to finish it.* Carlos' vision was clouded by fresh tears, and he wiped his eyes with his hand and began to read:

"My Dearest Carlos,

Words can't adequately describe the love I have for you. I thought we had more time together, but fate had other plans. We had so many plans, all the adventures we were going to have together. We were going to grow old together. Now, I understand that it was not meant to be. The realization is painful for me, but I am grateful for the time we have had together. I love you with all my heart, just as I have loved you since the day we met. My life with you has been better than I would have ever dreamed.

I am incredibly grateful for your friendship and your undying love. Being with you these past years was the greatest gift I could have been given.

You and I have built a life together that I've cherished, and I'm so thankful to you for the wonderful gift you have given me. I know you made sacrifices for me and our family and for that I'll be eternally grateful. Please, promise me that you will take care of yourself and our daughter, for my sake. Always remember that I'll always love and watch over you both. Finally, please don't forget the promise you made me.

Your love always, Lucy (H)"

Carlos folded the letter and placed it in his lap. Then he buried his head in his hands and wept.

4

Several weeks later, Assther and Carlos were driving home from school. Assther was deep in thought, gazing out the window. It had been a particularly long and difficult day. She'd returned to school a week ago and things weren't going well. All day, she couldn't shake the feeling that everyone's eyes were upon her. Increasingly, Assther had been thinking about what Aunt Judy had said. She was having difficulty sleeping and concentrating in class. Outside the car window, the sun was bright, and the rays dappled the hillside. Clouds hovered in clusters, casting shadows on the foothills.

Assther turned to her father and said, "Papi, did Mom have problems having kids?"

Suddenly, Assther noticed her father's jaw was clenched and he was gripping the steering wheel tightly. He cleared his throat repeatedly.

"What? What do you mean, mija?" he asked.

"I heard Aunt Judy saying something about Mom being unable to have kids. She was talking to one of her friends, and I overheard them after the funeral."

"I see," Carlos replied. He turned and smiled weakly at his daughter. For several minutes, there was a silence. "You took Sex Ed, right?" Carlos finally asked.

"Mm-hmm," responded Assther, turning her body in the seat to face her father.

"Did you cover the female anatomy?"

"Sort of," Assther replied, unsure of why her father asked.

"Your mother's uterus and fallopian tubes were blocked and not working properly. Despite having multiple surgeries to correct the problem, she was still unable have a baby." Carlos paused. "So we had to have a baby through a surrogate," he said.

"What's a surrogate?" Assther asked, more confused.

"A surrogate is a person who's willing to get pregnant for a family who can't have a baby on their own. That person carries the baby for the family."

Assther noticed her father's shoulders tense, and he shifted in the seat. Although Assther was observing her father, she didn't appreciate the change in his demeanor.

"Is that what happened with me? I was born through a surrogate?" Assther asked, looking at her father intently.

"Yes."

"Who's this woman? Was she my real mother?" Assther asked. As soon as the words passed through her lips, Assther regretted them. Although she was intrigued by what her father had just told her, she was also aware that her words had caused him a great deal of pain. Assther watched his body stiffen and his face contort.

"The woman worked for an agency," he said slowly. His voice was low, and there was an edge to it. "And your mother will always be your mother! I *don't* want to talk about this again." Having just arrived in front of the house, Carlos stopped the car, aggressively shifted into park, and shut off the engine. Then he exited the vehicle and slammed the car door shut behind him.

Assther watched her father retreat into the safety of their home. Sitting alone in the car, she considered the information she'd just heard. Her father was visibly distraught about the questions she was asking. Assther was uncertain if the issue of surrogacy or some other matter was the cause of his distress. It was apparent to Assther that she would need to investigate these subjects much more discretely and carefully in the future.

5

Later that evening, Assther decided it was time to read her mother's letter. She'd been unable to summon the courage to read it until her interaction with her father. Every time Assther considered it, she'd break into a cold sweat, and a wave of nausea would overtake her. However, after today, she realized she had no alternative. *Maybe this letter will give me more answers.*

While Assther was sitting on her bed holding her bear, Juki, she picked up the pink envelope and opened it slowly. The handwriting did not belong to her mother and Assther didn't recognize it. Assther exhaled deeply and began to read.

"My dearest Assther,

There are so many things that I want to tell you. So many things that I want to share with you. There'll be so many events in your life that I won't be able to be a part of or share with you. My heart breaks thinking about the advice I won't be able to impart to you, and it's too much to write in a single letter. I want you to know you've been a blessing to us since the moment you entered our lives. Your father and I have loved and cherished all the moments we've spent with you. I think back over the years and my heart is overflowing with joy. Assther, you're special and irreplaceable and destined for amazing things in the future. Although a part of me wishes I could see you fulfill your full potential, I've come to accept that it isn't meant to be. You'll decipher life's puzzles on your own, with your father's help. I've confidence in you. Please, have faith in yourself in those dark days when things appear hopeless. Please, take care of your father, he'll need you.

Always remember that I love you and will always be with you. Love always, Mom."

Tears cascaded down Assther's face as she held the letter close to her chest. Assther's heart was heavy with grief, and she felt a weakness in all her limbs. While reading the words, Assther could hear her mother's voice, and the realization that she would never hear her mother talk to her or sing with her again caused the wounds in her healing heart to reopen.

Special and irreplaceable, what does that mean? Assther wondered. There were more questions than answers, and Assther was more confused than before she'd begun reading her mother's letter.

Chapter 4

1

Born in Trinidad, a small town in central Cuba located on the Caribbean Coast, Carlos had been adopted by his maternal grandmother after his parents were killed in a car accident – caused by his drunk father. Carlos and his grandmother lived in a *barrio,* the poor section of town, in a one-bedroom apartment, which contained meager belongings and scant furniture. Growing up, Carlos contributed to the housekeeping, doing chores for his elderly grandmother and working odd jobs to help pay the bills.

As a teenager, Carlos' arms and legs grew long, making him tall and lanky with slim but athletic limbs. Painfully shy, Carlos assiduously avoided group activities, including sports; instead, he devoted hours reading books, losing himself in the places and characters about which he read.

When his friends were gathered in clubs, mastering the latest dances, like salsa and merengue and attempting to seduce the girls in town, Carlos would observe from a distance.

Since his interest in science had developed early, Carlos would spend hours watching his friends' interactions, taking notes on which couples were successful and which weren't.

Passionate about his studies, Carlos supplemented his education by learning multiple languages and other subjects which interested him. He dreamed of furthering his education by attending college in the United States. However, Carlos was reluctant to leave his grandmother behind.

After graduating from high school, Carlos received a full scholarship to the University of California in Berkeley. Carlos' grandmother had often told him she wanted him to get a quality education; she'd reiterated that he would be the first in the family to attend college, and she was proud of him. A few months later, Carlos prepared to relocate to California. Standing at the airport terminal, he felt ambivalent about leaving, seeing the tears spilling down his grandmother's weathered brown face. As Carlos said his tearful farewell to his beloved *abuelita*, he wasn't sure when or if they'd see each other again.

Initially after arriving in California, it was difficult for Carlos to adjust to a new environment, the people, and the country. Finally, in his sophomore year, Carlos developed a routine and felt more settled. He made some friends, his schoolwork was going well, and he was working and sending money to his grandmother back home.

At the end of his sophomore year, Carlos received a call that his *abuelita* had passed. She had had a stroke, and there was nothing they could have done to save her. After hearing the news, Carlos cradled the receiver in his hand and slid down the wall. It had been the two of them for so many years; his grandmother had been the source of kindness and encouragement; she'd become his mother. Despite their meager possessions, his grandmother had freely showered him with affection. Thinking back to their life together, Carlos became despondent at the profoundness of his loss; he realized he was all alone.

2

Living in a Jewish neighborhood in Brooklyn, Hannah's father was a teacher, and her mother worked at home raising the three girls. The family attended Shabbat, and High Holiday Services, and the girls prepared for their Bat Mitzvahs in Hebrew School.

Hannah, the youngest, and her mother could often be found baking together in the kitchen. During these times, Hannah's mother would impart motherly wisdom or baking tips, which Hannah cherished. While the two of them were alone in the kitchen, Hannah imagined herself in the future with her own daughter, bonding and baking.

Sharing a literary connection with her father, the two of them spent hours debating classical books. Her father was a patient and kind teacher, and he guided his youngest daughter through discourse and occasional spirited exchanges. Ensconced in the soft leather chair, Hannah sat in her father's study surrounded by the odor of books, which made her feel close to her father.

Moving to Berkeley as a freshman, Hannah was excited to study English literature and early childhood education. She was looking forward to meeting new friends and having new adventures.

3

"Vitameatavegamin," Hannah said.

Carlos and Hannah had met at a café on University Avenue for their first date. They each ordered coffee and a pastry and settled by the window of the shop.

Carlos didn't hear what Hannah had said.

"Huh?" Carlos said, taking a sip of his coffee.

"Didn't you ever see the show? I used to watch it with my parents." Hannah watched Carlos for several minutes and repeated, "Vitameatavegamin. It's from *I Love Lucy*."

"No," Carlos said. "We didn't have a television." He shifted in his seat and felt a rush of warmth filling his cheeks. Of course he'd heard of Ricky Ricardo and *I Love Lucy*. He braced himself for the inevitable question that was always asked, "Wasn't Ricky Ricardo also from Cuba?" Carlos wasn't sure why the only information people knew about Cuba was *I Love Lucy*, Castro, and Communism. Cuba, his beloved country, was so much more than that with the delicious food, diverse music, culture, and history. Carlos started to ache for his country, his beloved grandmother and her cooking. Oh, how he missed her.

"Maybe we can watch it together," Hanna said, tilting her head to the side coquettishly.

Carlos nodded mutely and looked at Hannah for several minutes. A glow in her face spread to her eyes and they danced like sparkling jewels. Although the coffee shop was loud and crowded, everyone suddenly disappeared. Only the two of them remained.

27

Hannah's fragrance–the scent of jasmine–wafted in his direction. *I would do anything with you,* he thought and smiled.

When Carlos was in Cuba, he'd studied his friends and their girlfriends, and how they behaved with each other. At that time, it was purely a scientific endeavor. Once, there had been a girl he'd liked and he'd tried to ask her out, but she made it clear she was only interested in being friends. It had been a heart-breaking lesson.

Carlos' reaction to Hannah surprised him. He'd never felt this way about a woman. It was as if he'd become intoxicated by an exotic substance that conquered him. It was clear that his life would be changed forever. Moving forward, he would do anything to make the woman sitting in front of him happy.

"Maybe I can call you Ricky?" Hannah asked.

"Only if I can call you Lucy," Carlos replied, winking.

4

Because of their hectic class schedules, Carlos and Hannah devised creative ways to find time to see each other. Low on funds, the couple took advantage of free shows, nature walks, and Saturday afternoon matinees – which were a treat. Their favorite places to visit were the UC Berkeley Botanical Garden and the redwood grove, which was located across the street.

In the early spring, Carlos and Hannah visited the immense UC Berkeley Botanical Garden. Meandering through the paths, they entered the California Area and saw cup-shaped bright-orange poppies and the hanging clusters of ivory urn-shaped flowers of the manzanitas resting on dark green foliage. Moving to the tropical house, there were delicate pink trumpet-shaped hibiscus. In the Chinese Medicinal Herb garden, Carlos pointed to stakes identifying and describing the various plants. Plump yellow and black striped bumble bees with pollen-caked proboscises zipped from plant to plant. A magenta-throated hummingbird droned nearby and seemingly in mid-air, luxuriated in the nectar from the fragrant island marrow tree. Hand in hand, Carlos and Hannah rested on a bench, enjoying the expansive view of the San Francisco skyline.

Over the next six months, Carlos and Hannah's relationship blossomed and deepened. The new sweethearts laughed, cried, argued, reconciled, and forged a powerful bond until they felt they were ready for the final step: marriage.

When Hannah informed her family in Brooklyn of the pending nuptials, they expressed their disapproval both on the basis of it being hasty, and especially because of Carlos' religious affiliation (he was not Jewish). Hannah reiterated to her family that she and Carlos were getting married regardless of any familial misgivings. Eventually, a compromise was reached, and Hannah's family acquiesced to the wedding.

5

On a bright, cloudless Sunday afternoon in June, the wedding party and guests gathered at Mather Redwood Grove and Townsend Amphitheater for Carlos' and Hannah's wedding ceremony. The towering Coastal Redwood trees with conical crowns and thick red bark provided an unforgettable venue for the celebration. The air was crisp, the ground was blanketed with lush green clover, and shafts of sunlight penetrated the canopy and dappled the leaves.

Wedding guests were seated in the half-moon shaped amphitheater with the evergreens soaring overhead. The magnificent trees gleamed as the sun's rays enveloped them. In front of the stage, a string quartet played a collection of wedding songs.

Wearing a sleeveless silk dress with the bodice embroidered with gems, Hannah's lace train trailed behind her. A floral diaphanous veil covered her delicate face and was secured to a headband. Hannah's long auburn hair was arranged in a tight bun and two spiral curls framed her face. While clutching a nosegay of fresh flowers in one hand, Hannah held her father's arm in the other. She ascended the stairs to the stage where a *chuppah* was festooned with ivory ribbons and tropical flowers. The guests rose as the string quartet began playing 'Entrance of the Queen of Sheba' by Handel.

Hannah joined her groom under the *chuppah*, and the rabbi began the ceremony. Surrounded by guests and family, Carlos and Hannah recited the ceremonial blessings. Then Carlos smashed the glass cup placed under his foot by the rabbi.

"Mazel Tov!" everyone cheered, as Carlos and Hannah were declared man and wife. Tenderly, Carlos kissed his new wife.

Taking his new bride's hand, Carlos gazed deep into her eyes and recited a poem from the *Song of Songs*:

"You have ravished my heart, my sister my bride! You have ravished my heart with one of your eyes, with one bead of your necklace.

How fair is your love, my sister my bride! How much better is your love than wine! And the smell of your ointments than all manner of spices!

Your lips, O my bride, drop honey—honey and milk are under your tongue; and the smell of your garments is like the smell of Lebanon.

A garden shut up is my sister, my bride, a spring shut up, a fountain sealed.

Your shoots are a part of pomegranates, with precious fruits: henna with spikenard plants,

Spikenard and saffron, calamus and cinnamon with all trees and frankincense: myrrh and aloes, with all the chief spices.

You are the fountain of gardens, a well of living water, and flowing streams from Lebanon.

Awake, O north wind; and come, you south; blow upon my garden, that the spices may flow out.[1]

While standing in the *chuppah*, Carlos gazed up and saw his bride enter. As he watched her, she seemed to glide toward him.

---

1 Song of Solomon 4:9–16

He felt a warmth in his heart and his breath catch as he lifted Hannah's veil. He couldn't believe she'd agreed to spend the rest of her life with him. Having selected the poem especially for her, Carlos had recited it in fluent Hebrew, then in English.

Carlos gazed at his new wife and felt the vastness of the universe becoming smaller with Hannah by his side. He made a pledge to all the gods in the heavens that he would use all his powers to protect Hannah and always ensure her happiness.

As Hannah approached Carlos standing under the *chuppah*, she felt nervous. She'd been unable to eat that morning because her stomach was flip-flopping. It had been painful for Hannah to defy her family about the wedding; she adored them and wanted nothing more than to please them. Nevertheless, she loved Carlos and wanted to build a life with him, and she was never more certain of anything in her life.

When she'd first met Carlos in the library, Hannah felt an instant connection with him. Now, his touch elicited an electrical reaction in her she could neither explain nor understand, but she knew it thrilled her. Just being near him made her feel strong, respected, and protected. Hannah envisioned a happy life with Carlos as their affection grew with time. Seeing the love in her new husband's eyes, Hannah smiled and knew this was the happiest day of her life.

6

Combining their meager finances and the money they'd received at the wedding, the newlyweds departed to Santa Cruz for their honeymoon. They rented a cozy one-bedroom apartment several blocks from the ocean. The space was furnished with wooden rattan furniture, which was covered with threadbare cushions, and the walls were decorated with various scenes of sea life. The bathroom fixtures were slightly rusted from the salty air. Through the open window, Hannah heard the ebb and flow of the ocean. Carlos and Hannah lounged for hours, listening to the calming sounds of the water.

Holding his bride in his arms, Carlos felt her soft body against his and drank in her jasmine scent. He felt complete happiness. At that moment there was nowhere else Carlos would rather be. Since the death of his beloved grandmother, Carlos had been lonely and bereft. A warm feeling was beginning to replace the emptiness that had pervaded his heart for so long. Carlos embraced his wife tightly and savored every moment.

The newlyweds spent the hot sun-drenched days at the beach, or on short trips to Monterey or Carmel. Carlos—a powerful swimmer, having grown up near a beach in Cuba—would rise early and swim in the ocean, allowing Hannah to sleep in. Later, they passed the day at the beach with a packed picnic, reading, swimming, and enjoying each other's company.

Leaning back against the beach chair, Hannah dug her toes into the warm sand and gazed out at the blue-green water. She had always found the rhythmic pounding of the waves soothing. As a child, Hannah's family vacationed on the beach each summer. She and her sisters frolicked in the seashore for hours. *The ocean in New York was much warmer,* Hannah thought with a slight shiver. The steady snoring of her companion brought her out of her reverie, and she turned to look at her husband.

His broad shoulders and muscular chest lifted with each breath. *How is it possible that I am so fortunate to be loved by someone like Carlos?* she wondered. He was brilliant by all accounts, athletic, good looking, and infinitely kind.

Prior to meeting Carlos, Hannah had had a boyfriend in high school; it had been short-lived. Hannah remembered feeling ignored and unappreciated. With Carlos, however, she felt treasured and respected. When they made love, he was patient and tender.

Hannah had not imagined she could ever love anyone the way she did Carlos. She glanced at his facial features and began to imagine what their children's characteristics and personalities would be. Hannah wanted to build a family with Carlos and, share the love with their child.

Hand in hand, Hannah and Carlos strolled down the shoreline as the salty ocean splashed their legs. The sun warmed their backs. Families nearby were gathered for barbecues. Children chased each other in and out of the water, squealing in delight. A group was playing volleyball, and two men in form-fitting Speedos tossed a frisbee back and forth. Hannah looked up and noticed a kite bobbing aimlessly against the cloudless blue sky. She smiled with contentment. *This will be a perfect place for a family vacation when Carlos and I have kids*, she thought.

While visiting the city of Carmel-by-the-Sea, Carlos and Hannah enjoyed a dinner in a romantic Italian restaurant. The candle on the corner table flickered as Carlos looked at his new bride. Patrons were conversing nearby, and the busboy was clearing the table next to them. Carlos felt fortunate to have Hannah in his life. On certain days, Carlos would watch his wife silently and marvel at the treasure he'd been gifted. His memory drifted to the first time they'd met. Carlos recalled the memory as if it was yesterday.

Carlos had begun working at UC Berkeley Moffitt Undergraduate Library so he could send money to his grandmother. Even after her death, Carlos continued to work there. He liked the job, the people were friendly, it was on campus, and he loved the feel and smell of the books.

During one of his shifts, Carlos was assigned to the information desk. He glanced up and noticed a woman approaching. Suddenly, events were occurring in slow motion. Carlos was mesmerized by her cherubic face and soft brown eyes.

"Excuse me," she whispered.

Carlos didn't hear her.

"Excuse me," she repeated, slightly louder and more insistently.

After moving his chair closer, Carlos said, "I'm sorry, I didn't hear you. Can I help you?"

She'd requested information about a book on English literature. Over the next several weeks, the same woman returned repeatedly. And she always asked Carlos for help.

Sometime later, Hannah returned to her dorm room after a visit to the library. As she retrieved one the books preparing to write her report, a piece of paper floated onto the floor. Hannah picked up the note.

"What's this?" she whispered and unfolded the paper.

It read:

How fine
you are, my love,
your eyes like doves
behind a veil.
Your hair-
as black as goats
winding down the slopes.
Your teeth-
a flock of sheep
rising from the stream
in twos, each with its twin.
Your lips-
like woven threads of crimson silk.[2]
Please have coffee with me, Carlos

Carlos grinned at the memory. He'd never done anything like that. Despite having read many romance novels, Carlos wouldn't call himself a romantic, more a pragmatist. He realized that about himself. But Carlos also understood if he hadn't attempted to connect with Hannah, he would've regretted it for the rest of his life.

Slowly, Carlos slid his hand on the linen tablecloth and grasped Hannah's hand.

"I was just thinking about how we met," he said in a soft voice.

The corners of Hannah's lips turned up into a broad smile, and her eyes sparkled.

---

2 Falk, M 2004 *The Song of Songs: Love Lyrics from the Bible*, 6th Edition, Brandeis University Press, Lebanon, NH

"You were pretty clever slipping that poem in with my books."

"Well, I had to do something different," Carlos said, lifting her hand to his lips. He kissed it tenderly.

"Hannah, I will love you forever," he said, and his blue eyes became very dark.

"I love you too, Carlos."

The night was balmy, and Carlos and Hannah strolled along a narrow path, which led to the beach. Having removed their shoes, the cool sand crunched under their bare feet. The scent of the salty spray of the ocean drifted towards them. Carlos and Hannah heard the crashing waves as they approached the shore. The wind rustled the leaves of the trees overhead as they laid their blanket down on the sand.

Sitting on the blanket and gazing up at the sky, they were treated to a spectacular planetary display of dazzling lights against an ebony backdrop. Carlos began pointing to stars and constellations and naming them.

"There's Capricornus and the Ursa Major," he said.

"What's that?" asked Hannah, pointing to a blinking light.

"That's a satellite," Carlos said, with a soft laugh.

Hannah reclined on the blanket, spread her arms out, and said, "I don't really care what they're called. This is beautiful! You never see the stars like this in the city."

They relaxed on the blanket in silence for a while, admiring the unlimited vista extending from one end of the horizon to the other.

"What do you think of inter-galactic travel?" Carlos asked, still looking up at the night sky.

"Well, I don't think the average person will be doing that in our lifetime," Hannah said. "Although I do like watching *Star Trek*." She turned and smiled at him.

Carlos lifted himself on his elbow and began tickling her side. "What is it with you and television shows?"

"Don't tell me you haven't see *that* show either," Hannah said between giggling breaths.

He bent down and kissed her gently and his kiss tasted salty. Hannah liked it.

Chapter 5

1

The honeymoon week ended quickly, and the newlyweds returned to Berkeley and to their new studio apartment as husband and wife. While Hannah was completing her degree in early childhood education and English literature, Carlos was working on his senior project with his two partners, Ivan Kaminsky and Allan Jackson. After moving to California, Carlos had been happy to find friends like them. Although the three of them came from different parts of the world, they became fast friends, and Carlos considered them part of his growing family. Meeting Hannah and his new friends helped Carlos feel more settled in his new home.

The three friends worked on their senior project under the direction of their adviser, Dr. Schmeck, who would be overseeing the endeavor for the next few years. Their project began to require more and more of their time including nights, evenings and weekends. This meant Carlos would be spending less time with Hannah.

Hannah was unsure if she should be jealous of the time Carlos was spending with his friends. Frequently, she teased her husband and said, "You guys are like the Three Musketeers."

Carlos sat and chewed the inside of his cheek in deep contemplation as he remembered the initial conversation he'd had with his two friends about Hannah. Carlos had informed them that he'd met her at the library ...

The three friends had met in a coffee shop to work on their project. They always sat at the back of the café so they wouldn't be disturbed. Not long after they were seated, Carlos sprang from his chair and frantically began pacing. His two friends watched his agitated demeanor in confusion.

After several minutes, Allan reached out and grabbed Carlos by the elbow. "Carlos, please sit down and tell us what's going on. You're making us very nervous."

Sighing heavily, Carlos perched on the edge of his chair and said, "I just met the most beautiful woman I've ever seen."

Ivan and Allan exchanged surprised glances. "What do you mean?" Ivan asked.

"When I was working my shift at the library, this woman approached the desk and asked for help." Carlos paused for several minutes. "Oh, I've never felt this way about anyone before." Carlos' face had a dreamy expression. "Then I asked her out and, you won't believe this" – he paused and his face flushed with excitement – "she said yes."

Allan and Ivan sat motionless for a few moments. "Carlos, you're aware this is impossible," Allan said gingerly.

Carlos turned to his friends slowly and replied, "I know it's not allowed, and it shouldn't have happened." His jaw was set in defiance, and his eyes were narrowed. "But I didn't expect it to happen. When I saw Hannah, it was as if the world itself shifted under me. I know the work we have to do requires complete commitment." Carlos hesitated for several minutes. "I also know that what I've found in Hannah I can't give up. It's too special, and I can't walk away."

"I hope you know what you're doing," Ivan said with a troubled expression on his face.

"I do," Carlos reassured his friends. "Don't worry, everything'll be fine." ...

Recently, Hannah was becoming emphatic about meeting Ivan and Allan. Carlos understood that he couldn't hold her off any longer.

"I'll cook everything. You just have to come, eat and drink. It'll be fun," Hannah said, looking at her husband eagerly.

Carlos didn't reply.

"Please, you spend so much time with them. I want to meet them and get to know them. I want to feel like I'm still a part of your life," she pleaded, her eyes welling up with tears.

His heart ached. How could he refuse her even though it was dangerous?

"Okay," Carlos said, "tomorrow evening. It's a date." With a heavy heart he kissed her on the cheek.

What have I done? Carlos thought.

2

After her classes the following afternoon, Hannah rushed home and prepared a three-course meal, which included shrimp cocktail, beef stroganoff, rice pilaf, and a side salad. For dessert, Hannah baked her signature red velvet cake, just like the one she used to bake with her mother.

Carlos entered their apartment, looked around the room, and exclaimed with a broad smile, "Honey, the food smells amazing!"

"Thank you."

"The cake looks exquisite," Carlos said. "I think it's one of your best." He handed her a bouquet of flowers. "I love you," he whispered in her ear and kissed her gently on the lips.

The cozy apartment had a mixture of the aroma from the food Hannah had prepared and a scented candle she had lit. Hannah walked to the record player, selected a record, and placed it onto the turntable. After gently depositing the needle into the groove, she listened for the throaty vocals of Diana Krall. Then, surveying the scene, she smiled with satisfaction and said, "I think we're ready."

At seven o'clock, their small apartment was ready to receive guests. The fresh flowers were arranged in a crystal vase, the dining room table was set for four, a black cherry candle was burning, and Cabernet Sauvignon was decanted and ready to pour. Hannah had to admit she was excited and slightly nervous.

The first guest arrived at one minute past seven. *Very punctual*, thought Hannah. She opened the door and saw an athletic man with platinum blond hair and piercing blue eyes–similar to her husband's. Hannah's eyes grew wide.

"Hi, Hannah. I'm Ivan," he said and smiled at her.

She recovered quickly and became the consummate host. "Hi, Ivan, nice to meet you. Please come in," she said. "Would you like a drink before dinner?"

"Yes, thank you," Ivan replied as he entered the apartment and situated himself on the futon/couch—which also doubled as Hannah and Carlos' bed.

"Carlos, could you get the wine—" *ding, dong*

Hannah moved to the door and opened it.

"Hi, Hannah. I'm Allan," he said and handed Hannah a bottle of Jose Cuervo. He was a muscular African American man with intense blue eyes. Hannah had to steady herself on the door frame.

"Please come in, Allan," Hannah said weakly. "Ivan and Carlos are inside." Hannah shut the door and exhaled deeply. She studied the bottle she was handed. *This is going to be interesting.*

Hors d'oeuvres had been arranged on the glass coffee table, and the three men sat on the couch conversing cheerfully.

Standing nearby, Hannah poured herself a glass of wine and observed the trio.

"Allan, I understand from Carlos that you grew up in Miami?" Hannah asked, taking a sip of her wine.

"That's right," Allan answered. "Have you ever been?"

"No. I understand it's a beautiful place."

A dreamy expression floated over Allan's face. "Oh yes. If you were in space and looked down at the city, it would sparkle like a jewel." He paused and added, "It's the vibrant people, music and culture. It's as if the air was suffused with a certain energy."

Carlos and Ivan exchanged glances and shifted in the couch.

"That sounds amazing," Hannah said, her eyebrows lifting. Then she looked at Ivan, who was delicately placing a cracker and cheese sandwich into his mouth. Hannah observed him as he raised his wine glass to his nose, sniffed the aroma, and finally sipped the wine.

"And Ivan, how are you adjusting to the Bay Area?" Hannah asked.

"It's definitely not Minsk," Ivan said. "In fact, the first few months, I was walking around in shorts and a T-shirt when others were wearing coats. Looking back, I'm sure people must have thought I was crazy."

Hannah nodded mutely and took another sip of wine.

"Well, gentlemen, dinner's ready. Shall we all sit down?"

After they began eating, Hannah studied the three men. She could not understand what was unfolding in front of her, and her thoughts were racing. Certainly, it could be a coincidence, but she didn't believe in coincidences. Was this the reason her husband didn't want her to meet his friends? What secret was her husband hiding which could explain what she was observing? She experienced a momentary alarm. Could she be in some kind of danger?

For Hannah, the dinner progressed poorly, and she ate very little. When the men complimented her cooking and the décor, she nodded absentmindedly. Hannah passed the evening comparing the three men's features, her eyes bouncing between each man. She wasn't sure if it was only the color of their eyes that was similar. Was she also noticing similar mannerisms and facial features? Their laugh, the curves of their chins, and shape of their noses were also oddly similar. Hannah was trying to solve a puzzle for which she didn't have all the pieces.

Those three could be triplets, she thought. *But how? They come from different parts of the world!*

The three men, on the other hand, were unaware of Hannah's distress; they were enjoying the food, the alcohol, and each other's company. Occasionally, Carlos would glance over at his wife and notice her troubled facial expression. He would feel a knot form in the pit of his stomach. As the evening progressed, Carlos realized he would have to provide his wife an explanation.

Later that night, while Carlos and Hannah were in bed, Hannah hesitantly asked her husband to explain. Staring at the their apartment's popcorn ceiling, Carlos tried to find a way to clarify the situation and still keep his wife safe.

Chapter 6

1

Having finally graduated with their college degrees, Carlos and Hannah moved to a bigger apartment. Carlos started working on his master's degree at UC Berkeley while Hannah worked with preschoolers. Both felt like they were utilizing their education and establishing themselves.

Several months later, Hannah began to feel the urge to nest. Carlos surprised Hannah with a fish tank and some assorted tropical fish. He explained that it would be a way to *ease them into parenthood*. After the fish survived, they decided to adopt a tuxedo cat from the shelter. They named him Cosmo–after their favorite character on Seinfeld. Cosmo adapted quickly to his new home, often burrowing between the two of them on the futon/bed to purr happily and nap while they lounged together to watch TV.

Hannah would observe the animal in its ritual ablution and marvel how the pink tongue glossed over the fur. After finishing the ritual, Cosmo moved close to Hannah, curled into a ball, and slept. Hannah enjoyed watching his behavior and having his soft, warm body near her.

A few months later, while Carlos and Hannah were in bed with Cosmo wedged between them purring, Hannah turned to Carlos and told him she was ready to start a family. Carlos surveyed their cramped apartment, the cat, and the fish tank.

After several minutes, he looked at his beloved and said, "How about we start now?" He smiled and kissed her tenderly on the lips.

In the beginning, trying to conceive was fun for Carlos and Hannah. However, after a year, Hannah became discouraged and disheartened regardless of Carlos' efforts to improve her mood. They turned to friends for advice on various sexual positions, ovulation kits, even internet sites for vitamins to optimize conception. Finally, they realized it was time to seek professional help.

After they both had blood tests and scans, the doctors informed them that Hannah was born with an abnormally formed uterus and her fallopian tubes were blocked. Although Hannah underwent several surgical procedures, they were told their chances of conception were low.

After hearing the news from the doctors, Hannah began to see children everywhere she went: while driving, in the park, being pushed by their parents–their miniature feet peeking out of strollers, toddlers running to their mothers, and babies in high-chairs in restaurants. At times, she sat in her car for hours in front of coffee shops observing parents with their children.

The growing yearning for a child was intensifying daily, and Hannah was losing her ability to function. Her job, which entailed working with kindergarteners, became impossible for her to continue.

Becoming further dispirited, Hannah took to her bed, refusing to eat or go to work. Laundry and dishes began piling up, and there was no food in the house. Hannah didn't care. Usually fastidious about her appearance, it would be days between bathing or brushing her teeth. All of Carlos' efforts to improve her spirits proved futile. Cosmo refused to leave Hannah's side and would burrow and sleep for hours next to her.

2

"You look awful," Ivan exclaimed one morning as Carlos walked into work. The three friends were working together at a bio-medical engineering company on a cutting-edge project, along with their adviser, Professor Schmeck. The immense room in which they worked was a converted warehouse and required the temperature to be maintained at sixty-two degrees for their research. Regardless of the weather outside, the employees wore pants and sweaters to keep warm. The concrete floor had been covered with thin, easy to clean linoleum, which added to the frigidity of the room. Multiple computer stations had been installed along with various electronic equipment. Cameras were situated in each corner, and access into the facility was only permitted through an optical scanner.

Carlos had dark circles around his eyes, and his hair was even wilder than usual.

"I haven't been sleeping well," he said.

"Hannah still isn't doing well?" Ivan asked with a worried expression.

"No, she's not eating or sleeping." Carlos sat down at his desk in front of the computer and sighed heavily. "We've seen the doctor and she's tried multiple medications for depression. But she can't tolerate them." Carlos' forehead was lined with worry.

Ivan, who had been working at his desk across the room, walked the length of the lab. His footsteps echoed on the polished floor. He sat down on a bench next to his friend and asked, "How can we help?"

"I don't know," Carlos said. "Now the cat isn't eating, either. I can't even coax it to eat." He cupped his head in his hands. "I just don't know what to do anymore!"

Carlos felt increasingly helpless watching Hannah's condition deteriorate and seeing her languish in bed all these months. He was resolved to fight for them both because his love for her wouldn't allow him to simply surrender.

After approaching Carlos from his workstation, Allan placed a hand on his shoulder and said, "I'm sorry, amigo. Please tell us how we can help."

Suddenly, Carlos jumped up. He had a determined expression in his eyes.

"Carlos, whatever you're thinking about doing, don't do it. It'll end badly," Ivan said, observing his friend with apprehension.

Ivan and Allan exchanged worried glances.

"I have to do something. I can't lose her!"

"Carlos, please don't do it," Allan said, his voice tense. "Schmeck won't like it."

Carlos looked at each of his friends and in a calm tone said, "I have *no* choice." He squared his shoulders, straightened his back, and walked briskly out of the lab.

3

While Hannah continued to struggle, Cosmo kept her company. His soft black fur and vibrating body provided her only minimal comfort. Hannah remained in bed unable to shake her depression and get back to Carlos, work, and life. None of the medication she had tried had helped her, and she was worried she might never be able to escape the darkness in which she currently found herself. The drugs made Hannah feel worse than she had before she started taking them.

She and Carlos had even discussed adoption, but they were told they would need to wait up to two years. Hannah wanted to be a mother with every fiber of her being; to nurture, raise and share her knowledge with another being was what she was destined to do.

Hannah had learned the precious bond of motherhood from her mother, and she was ready to be one. Certainly she knew there would be difficulties; she anticipated them and was prepared and even anxious for them. All Hannah wanted was a lifeline to return her to the light and help her battle for herself and her family.

These were Hannah's thoughts a month later when Carlos returned home and handed her a small bundle wrapped in a white blanket.

"Meet Assther," Carlos said softly, bending down and handing his wife the blanketed package.

Hannah took the bundle hesitantly. Peeking inside, she was shocked to find a newborn baby staring up at her.

As soon as Cosmo saw the baby, his tail fanned out like a pipe cleaner, and he gave a low, guttural growl and hiss and scampered under the bed.

"Is she ..." Hannah asked in disbelief, not taking her eyes off the child.

"Yes."

Hannah could not believe it. The two perfect eyes, delicate fingers and toes. The perfect nose and the angelic features. She touched the baby's face gently to confirm that it was real, and she was not dreaming; she was not dreaming. Hannah pulled the bundle close and gingerly kissed her little face; it was warm and smelled like candy, Hannah thought.

Hannah could not believe such joy was possible. She looked deeply into her daughter's eyes. Hannah vowed she would always protect her child and promised to love her as long as she lived.

As Hannah was gazing into her daughter's eyes, she saw her lifeline and tentatively grasped it. With tears flowing from her eyes, Hannah slowly began the long process of clawing her way back from the abyss in which she had been living. *My daughter*, she thought, *my baby*. Hannah didn't know how or from where Carlos brought Assther, but she was sure that he hadn't done anything illegal.

Because he's a good man, she thought.

Looking into her husband's eyes, Hannah knew that she was right.

With tears gathering in his eyes, Carlos watched his new family for several minutes and kissed them both. Hannah began bonding with Assther, and he knew that with time his beloved would recover and come back to him. Carlos sighed softly. *Whatever happens, it was worth it*, Carlos thought. His commitment to her had deepened, and he was prepared to endure any consequences from his actions.

Chapter 7

1

Being a mother came naturally for Hannah, and she enjoyed every aspect of motherhood. Her dreams of being a mother had come true, and she was happy spending time with her daughter. Carlos would come home from work and exclaim, "Lucy, I'm home!" and find the aroma from Hannah's latest creation permeating the house.

Unfortunately, Cosmo never adapted to Assther. He would growl and hiss or wail continuously whenever he saw her. Carlos and Hannah were unable to find the cause of his distress, despite extensive testing by the vet. Eventually, they had to give him to a neighbor, who agreed to adopt him. Heartbroken, Hannah would visit Cosmo regularly.

Under the love and guidance of both her parents, Assther was blossoming into a beautiful and smart child. She loved reading books with Carlos, singing songs and playing dress-up or tea-time with Hannah, and spending time together just the three of them.

Hannah and Assther would spend their days together at the park, reading or playing games. At home in the afternoons, while looking up intermittently from her reading, Hannah would watch Assther draw exquisite pictures. As Assther grew, Hannah would focus on her daughter's features and consider her intellect. Hannah's eyes would become misty when she considered the activities they had shared and would share together.

Hannah felt indebted to Carlos for bringing Assther home that day. Every time she recalled that time in her life, Hannah's stomach would twist into a knot; she was sure that without Assther, her life would've turned out differently. Hannah was grateful to her daughter for rescuing her from doom. But on certain sleepless nights, she tossed and turned, tormented by the thought of what price she and Carlos would have to pay for the salvation. In vain, Hannah would repeatedly attempt to drive these thoughts out of her mind.

2

"Hello, *familia*, I'm home," Carlos called out as he entered the house after a long day of work.

"We're in the kitchen, honey," Hannah replied.

Carlos followed the sound of laughter and entered the kitchen to find his wife and ten-year-old daughter covered in flour. The kitchen was in complete disarray; cake pans and baking ingredients were scattered all over the counter, and there was spillage on the floor.

"Another afternoon of baking?" Carlos asked, surveying the scene in amusement.

"Yes." Hannah beamed. These days baking with Assther reminded her of the times she used to spend with her own mother. Hannah enjoyed seeing Assther's face as the two of them measured, mixed, and scooped the batter into the final creation.

"Guess what we're making today, Papi?" Assther asked excitedly.

"Chocolate chip and cucumber cookies?" Carlos asked as he placed his briefcase on the floor.

"Right. How did you know?" Assther asked.

He smiled and gave his daughter a kiss on her forehead, the only location without any flour.

"I guess I'm the guinea pig again tonight?" he asked and winked at his daughter.

Carlos looked at his wife, his brow furrowed, and asked, "It's the same recipe again?"

"Yes," Hanna said. "She wanted to make it again. Why?" Hannah's smile faded abruptly.

"Assther, why don't you go upstairs and get cleaned up for dinner?" Carlos said.

"Okay," replied Assther, cheerfully grabbing her bear, Juki, who had been resting on the counter. She bounded up the stairs to her room.

Hannah gave her husband a suspicious look and asked, "Carlos, what's going on? Are you concerned that Assther has asked to make the same recipe all week?"

"I'm sure it's nothing. Do you need help cleaning the kitchen?"

"No, I can take care of it," Hannah reassured him, scrutinizing him closely.

Hannah watched Carlos as he walked toward his office. While scrubbing the flour and stuck-on egg particles from the granite countertop with a wet rag, Hannah contemplated her husband's words. *Why was he troubled by Assther's choice of cookie recipes?* Hannah wondered. *Is there something I need to be concerned about as well? Is there something wrong with Assther?*

After entering his dark office in the back of the house, Carlos turned and perched at the edge of his desk. He lowered his head and closed his eyes in deep concentration. After a short time, he reached for the desk lamp and flicked it on. Then he picked up the receiver on his desk phone and dialed a number.

"Hi, Ivan," Carlos said. "It's Carlos." As he spoke, he skirted the desk and sat in the leather chair. "I need your help."

"Okay, Carlos," Ivan said. "Is everything all right?"

"There's a malfunction in the program, and I can't figure it out." Carlos hesitated, taking a deep breath. "I need help to find the problem."

"Of course, Carlos. Perhaps it's the interface between the two technologies. We can work on it tomorrow together."

"Thank you, Ivan," replied Carlos, turning on his computer. "I'll see you tomorrow."

3

Several months later, the family was preparing to have dinner when the phone rang.

"Hello … Yes, I'll be right there," Carlos said after picking up the phone. He was pale and appeared visibly shaken. He kissed his wife and told her he would be back in a few hours. Hannah and Assther ate dinner without him.

Carlos and Ivan had arranged to meet at Allan's apartment. Carlos arrived first and entered using the spare key Allan had given him years before. The apartment was unchanged, typical bachelor décor with a large screen television as the centerpiece and other furniture built around it: wraparound couch, large speakers, and a gaming console.

The apartment was tidy, and Carlos remembered that Allan had a weekly cleaning service. Carlos walked into Allan's bedroom, which was chaotic, his bed in disarray, clothes strewn about on the floor. While checking the wooden armoire, Carlos saw a row of brand-new tailored gray and black suits beside starched white and blue dress shirts. *These must be for his new job. He only wore jeans and sweaters when we worked together,* thought Carlos. *I should've reach out to him after the last meeting.*

With a deep sigh, Carlos sat on the corner of the unmade bed. He recalled the first time he'd met Allan during freshman orientation at UC Berkeley. Allan was frequently making jokes in an attempt to make others laugh. During their freshman year, Allan had confided in Carlos that he was actually extremely shy and an introvert. Also, he hated jokes. Allan explained that when he was in high school, he was one of only two black students.

Because Allan's parents, both lawyers, wanted him to get the best education, they'd enrolled him at an elite high school. Allan had quickly discovered that humor, but jokes especially, disarmed people and allowed him to enter segments of society he wouldn't have been allowed into otherwise. He also realized that his jokes made him less threatening. Since freshman year, Allan's jokes became less frequent as he became increasingly comfortable expressing his authentic personality.

Carlos buried his head in his hands; he would miss his friend immensely. Why hadn't he reached out after the meeting? Allan had been very angry, and the supervisor was very unhappy with Allan's remarks.

"Carlos, are you here?" Carlos heard Ivan's voice calling from the hallway.

"In the bedroom," he answered feebly.

"Have you been here long?" Ivan asked, entering the bedroom.

"No," Carlos said, "just a little while." Carlos looked up at his friend and asked, "What did you find out?"

"I went to the scene of the accident" – Ivan paused – "and I spoke to the police. Apparently, Allan's car hit the guardrail at high speed." Ivan took a moment to stabilize his quivering voice.

"Did you see the ..." Carlos could not allow himself to finish the sentence.

"No," replied Ivan somberly. "They had taken him away before I got there."

Ivan sat down next to his friend and placed his arm on his shoulder. After a few minutes of silence, Ivan asked, "Do you think this accident has anything to do with what happened that day at the office? All those things Allan had said?"

"I don't know," Carlos replied gravely.

The two men sat quietly for several minutes, each lost in his own thoughts. After a while, Carlos turned to his companion and asked, "What do you think of what Allan was saying?" he hesitated. "What do you think about his theory?"

Ivan took a deep breath before responding, "You mean Allan's theory that we were fired because Shimizu is now working with the government?"

Carlos nodded silently.

"I'm not sure I believe it," Ivan said.

"Well," Carlos said, rubbing his eyes, "if it's true, I don't think it'll end well. And I think we need to be very careful from now on."

When Carlos returned home several hours later, Hannah could see the pain in his eyes.

"Carlos, where were you? What happened?" Hannah asked.

"Allan is dead," Carlos explained. His blue eyes looked like the ocean with a hurricane brewing. "Apparently there was a car accident."

"Honey, I'm so sorry." Hannah was silent for a few minutes. "Do you know what happened?" She sat next to her husband and put her hand on his arm.

"The only thing they know is that Allan was involved in a car accident and that he's dead."

Abruptly, Carlos stood up, started pacing and wringing his hands.

"According to the police, his car was driving very fast and hit the guardrail. He was pronounced dead at the scene." Carlos' face was distorted.

He stopped pacing and was staring into the distance.

"Do you think it has anything to do with what happened at your work? You told me Allan had been very upset."

Carlos perched at the edge of the chair and softly said, "I really don't know." He took a deep breath. "We were all upset."

"Wasn't Allan furious at Schmeck, too?" Hannah asked tentatively. "Did you talk to Dr. Schmeck? Does he know anything?"

"Hannah, I don't know," Carlos said and stood up. "I'm tired." He kissed her softly on the cheek and walked slowly out of the room.

Chapter 8

1

The years passed and Assther grew into a beautiful young woman with raven hair that fell in ringlets around her face. Hannah would observe her daughter with some nostalgia as they ate breakfast together. Since Assther had started high school last year, she'd become so much more independent. Hannah recalled the days when it was just the two of them; the days she would dress Assther in adorable dresses with matching shoes, and arrange her hair a special way. Then arrived the bittersweet days when Assther announced she no longer needed Hannah's help picking clothes or fixing her hair. Hannah mentally ran through the milestones. *Those days are over.*

Watching her daughter become a woman, Hannah was becoming aware that she and Carlos would be empty nesters soon. She would've loved to have another child, but she didn't share her feelings with Carlos; he'd sacrificed so much bringing Assther into their lives. Hannah cherished all the times she'd spent with her daughter, and it pained her that their special time together was coming to an end.

The changes Hannah was experiencing with Assther, and the notion she was losing her daughter had resurrected some of her old feelings. In the past few months, Hannah felt the old darkness begin to creep back and attempt to drag her back to the abyss. But she was able to suppress the emotions and fight back to the light.

As Assther was getting ready for school one morning, Hannah was seated at the kitchen table. After taking a sip of water, Hannah looked at her daughter and asked, "How's school?"

"Fine," Assther replied and poured her corn flakes into a bowl.

"Any tests today?" Hannah persisted.

"No," Assther said between bites. "Not today." Glancing up from her cereal, Assther suddenly stopped eating and asked, "Aren't you going to eat breakfast?"

"No. I'm not hungry now," Hannah replied and exhaled. "I'll eat later," she added and smiled faintly.

"Are you feeling okay? You haven't been eating the last few mornings," Assther asked with a worried expression on her face.

Hannah felt her lower abdomen seize her, and she grasped the corners of the wooden kitchen table with her fingers. "Of course, why wouldn't I be?" she replied and bit her lower lip. She forced her voice to remain steady. "You're going to be late for school. Have a good day." Hannah watched her daughter rush out the front door. *It's time!* Hannah told herself.

2

A few days later, Hannah was in the examination room wearing a paper gown waiting for the doctor to enter. The odor of antiseptic permeated the room, and she felt cold and exposed. Draping her sweater over her shoulders, Hannah studied the room. On the wall she saw a poster of a yellow tabby kitten hanging on to a tree with one paw that read 'Hang in there baby!' *If that's their attempt at humor,* Hannah thought, *it's not working.* On a metal stand near the examination table, there was a tray with a metal speculum and other supplies. Although Hannah had undergone the same examination in the past, somehow this time it was different. She knew her pain would increase during the examination. Part of her knew she needed to know the truth, and another was terrified of what it would mean to her and her family if something was actually wrong with her.

"Hello, Hannah," Dr. Acosta said after he entered the room. A petite nurse followed close behind. "I understand you've been having some pain."

Hannah nodded mutely, wrapping her sweater tighter.

"Well," the doctor said, sitting down on the stool, "let's take a look."

The nurse helped Hannah position her feet into the stirrups and instructed her to slide down. While Hannah was lying on the examination table, she was trying to take control of her imagination. She heard the doctor give instructions to the nurse. As the examination progressed, Hannah gripped the sides of the cold metal table with both hands and breathed heavily.

Hannah wished she was anywhere else, instead of on that cold, hard table. And she wished the probing was being performed on somebody else. Desperately, she wanted the discomfort she was experiencing to end.

The probing sent her spasms to a new high, and Hannah took deep breaths in a futile attempt to ease them. *Something must be really wrong*, Hanna thought. *This isn't normal*. Allowing the tears to fall freely relieved Hannah's pain only slightly. Finally, the examination was finished, the duo retreated behind the white door, and Hannah was instructed to dress. She was told the doctor would be back to talk with her.

Dismounting slowly, Hannah gently cleaned the gel from between her legs and pulled her clothes back on. She was grateful she'd worn her soft fleece sweatpants this morning. Perched on the edge of a chair, Hannah tried to find a comfortable position. Patiently, she waited until the doctor entered.

3

By the time Hannah returned home from her doctor's appointment, Carlos and Assther were busy preparing dinner. They didn't notice Hannah slip into the house and quickly rush up the stairs. Prior to coming into the house, Hannah had been sitting in the car for over a half an hour trying to summon the courage to enter. She knew she would have to share the news with her family.

"I'll be right down," Hannah shouted from the second floor, trying to keep her voice from breaking.

In her bedroom, Hannah sat on the edge of the bed and tried to pull herself together. After taking several deep breaths, she walked to the make-up table and sat down. She applied concealer and fixed her makeup. Then slowly, she descended the stairs and joined her family.

During dinner, which consisted of tacos and rice with salad, Assther recounted her day in school. The aroma of the food permeated the air. Both Carlos and Assther were enjoying the meal and chatting.

Holding the fork in his hand, Carlos stopped eating and observed his wife for several minutes. She was moving the food around her plate in a circular motion. Concerned, Carlos touched his wife's hand gently and asked, "Honey, are you okay? Aren't you hungry? You love it when I make this dish."

Hannah sat motionless and continued to stare into her plate.

After resting his fork on the table, Carlos turned toward his wife and repeated more urgently, "Hannah, what's wrong?"

Sitting at the dining room table, Hannah was unable to continue to pretend that she was fine. Her stomach was in knots, and she felt an overwhelming sense of dread. Hannah needed to unburden herself and share the potentially devastating news. Desperately, she hoped her family's love and support would help her.

"I went to the doctor today —" Hannah said, tears filling her eyes.

"Why?!" they both interrupted in unison.

"Because of my stomach pain. It's been getting worse and I didn't want to —" Hannah sighed heavily.

"How long have you been having this pain?" interrupted Carlos again, his brow furrowed and eyes narrowed.

"Six months," Hannah responded in a subdued voice, her eyes downcast.

"Six months!" Carlos pushed back his chair and jumped up. The women watched as he began pacing furiously in the kitchen. Back stiff and shoulders tense, Carlos' face was lined with worry.

"Carlos," Hannah pleaded, "please, don't be angry with me. I thought the pain would get better." She took a deep breath. "You were so busy with work I didn't want to worry you." She paused. "Assther has been doing so well at school and working too." Fresh tears streamed down her face. *How do I tell him that I might have cancer?* Hannah thought.

Assther moved to the chair previously occupied by Carlos, gently took her mother's hand, and softly asked, "Mom, what did the doctor say?"

Hannah looked at her daughter for several minutes, collecting her thoughts. "He said we need to run some tests."

Hearing the conversation, Carlos stopped pacing, spun around, and fell to his knees in front of his wife. Then he placed his head in Hannah's lap, and she stroked his hair gently and rhythmically.

"Everything'll be fine," Hannah reassured her family. They clung to each other, each thinking about how life would never be the same again.

Chapter 9

1

Dr. Rajah sat in front of the computer and reviewed her patient's chart. She leaned back in her chair to stretch, extending her lean frame. This would be her last patient for the day. *It has been a long day, and a long week*, she thought. She rubbed her temples, trying to increase the circulation to her brain. Reviewing the records, Dr. Rajah saw that the patient was young and had extensive disease. Having practiced oncology for many years, she was aware these types of cases were always difficult to treat.

Entering the cramped examination room, Dr. Rajah found Hannah sitting on the table with her hands on her lap. The husband and daughter were sitting nearby. Dr. Rajah introduced herself to each member of the family in turn. There was apprehension and concern on their faces.

After moving to the computer monitor located in the corner of the room, Dr. Rajah swiped her badge over a sensor to unlock it. Then she began typing rapidly. Finding Hannah's chart, Dr. Rajah perched on a stool and swiveled to face the family.

"How are you feeling after your surgery, Hannah?" Dr. Rajah asked with a smile.

"It's been two weeks now. I'm feeling stronger, and the pain has been improving," Hannah said.

"I'm glad to hear that." *Here comes the bad news*, thought Dr. Rajah. Although she'd been telling cancer patients their diagnoses for years, it still didn't get easier. Dr. Rajah pushed her fatigue aside and took a deep breath. Then she turned to her computer monitor and accessed the blood tests and pathology report.

"Your blood tests came back normal," she said, looking at her patient. "As you know, the surgeon removed your ovaries, uterus, appendix, and lymph nodes and sent samples to the pathologist for evaluation." All three nodded mutely. At this point, Dr. Rajah always made sure she used simple words and spoke slowly.

"This was done both to remove any cancer and to help us figure out what the best treatment plan should be," she continued, glancing over at the pathology report. "The pathology showed you have epithelial ovarian carcinoma."

In her years of practice, Dr. Rajah had seen a wide range of reactions from her patients, from mute catatonia to hysterical wailing, and she always prepared herself.

"What is the exact diagnosis?" Carlos asked, looking directly at Dr. Rajah.

Dr. Rajah shifted on her stool her and responded, "Stage IIIB epithelial ovarian carcinoma with ovarian primary." Then she looked at each of them in turn and said, "I want to assure you that you're not alone. We have a multidisciplinary team consisting of doctors, nurses, social workers, nutritionists, and therapists who'll help you through this process. You can count on us for any questions you may have." Instinctively, Dr. Rajah stood up and handed a box of tissues to Hannah.

Crying softly and taking a tissue to dab her eyes, Hannah asked, "What's the next step?"

"You'll need to start chemotherapy," Dr. Rajah replied softly. Hearing the information, Carlos stood up and began pacing.

After several minutes, Carlos asked, "Tell me, Doctor, what's my wife's prognosis?"

"We don't like to think in those terms—"

"Please, Dr. Rajah," he interrupted with an anxious tone.

"The five-year survival rate is 41.5 percent," replied the doctor in a subdued tone, looking in his direction.

Carlos melted into a chair.

Chapter 10

1

After her diagnosis, Hannah resolved not to allow her old feelings to overtake her; she would fight for her life and her family just as Carlos had done for her all those years ago. Her new perspective gave her more courage to face the future and plan for it, whatever the future would bring.

"There it is," Hannah said.

On a beautiful Sunday afternoon in May, Hannah and Carlos were driving, and she pointed to a large maple tree, which was in full bloom displaying its verdant crown on the hillside. It was surrounding by lush rolling hills.

Several weeks before on her last visit to Nana Ruth's gravesite, Hannah had discovered the tree while she'd had been strolling around the grounds. The tree was located on a grassy knoll surrounded by gravestones. Hannah had spent several hours under that tree. While reclining against its thick trunk, she had decided that in the event that she didn't survive, she needed to plan ahead.

As the tears flowed freely, Hannah watched butterflies flit aimlessly from flower to flower. In her mind's eye she pictured her family visiting that tree to recount their life stories, graduations, weddings, and other special events. Hannah had decided it would be her way of continuing to be a part of their lives and easing their sorrow. In a way, preparing for the possibility of death eased the anguish she was experiencing, giving her back some control over her life.

Now, it was a cloudless day and the wind carried the aroma of lavender in the air. Large bumblebees were gorging on the pollen of spring flowers, emitting a low buzz. Carlos and Hannah lingered in front of the tree for a few minutes.

Then Carlos nodded and continued driving. Moments later, they were at the front desk of the office asking to see the director. The place was poorly ventilated, with large faux leather chairs and a wooden podium. The unmistakable odor of mothballs and must permeated the air. Elevator music was piped into the room; Hannah hated elevator music.

"I'm the director. Can I help you?" answered a stocky gentleman with thinning black hair and a button nose. He was wearing an ill-fitting black suit and a disposable name tag upon which was written 'George/Manager,' in block letters.

After a brief explanation, the manager led them through the building to his desk. In the hallway, there were muted paintings of bygone pastoral scenes encased in elaborately engraved wooden frames. A heavy door was partially ajar and Hannah noticed a room filled with a variety of caskets displayed on metal pedestals.

Hannah imagined Dracula pushing the lid open with his ghostly hand and emerging from one of the wooden, lacquered coffins after his daily slumber. The corners of her lips lifted into a slight smirk.

"It's a good idea the two of you are looking for a final resting place early. Although it's going to be years before it'll be needed," George said and smiled at both of them in turn after they sat down.

"I'm dying of cancer," Hannah said. "So I'll be needing it pretty soon." No one spoke for several minutes.

"I'm sorry to hear that," George responded finally, his smile fading and the blood running to his already ruddy face.

"Don't be sorry," Hannah said. "You didn't give me cancer." She was becoming more disinhibited since her diagnosis, and she liked it.

"I'm trying to get things taken care of so my family" – she reached for Carlos' hand – "doesn't have to worry about it if and when I'm gone –"

"Excuse me, where's your restroom?" Carlos pushed his chair back and rushed toward where George was pointing. When he returned, his blue eyes were streaked red.

"How's Hannah doing?" asked Ivan a few weeks later while he and Carlos were eating lunch together.

"She started chemo, which is making her sick," Carlos said. "Assther and I are trying to keep her strength up." He paused. "I'm worried about Assther because she hasn't told any of her friends about her mother's illness. I don't think she's processing it properly." Carlos looked at his friend.

The smell of the chicken chow mein was making Carlos nauseous and, finally giving up, he released his fork.

"How are *you* doing?" Ivan asked in between bites of his sandwich.

Carlos stared mutely at his food.

"Carlos, you don't look good," Ivan said. "I'm worried about you. Are you eating and sleeping? You need to keep up your strength." Ivan had stopped eating and looked at his friend.

Carlos was silent for several minutes, and his gaze was distant. When he finally spoke, his voice was barely audible and quivering.

"Don't you understand, I don't care about myself!" He paused to regain control. "I would gladly give my life for hers if it would save her! I only care about Hannah and Assther. My one and only responsibility is to protect them, and I've failed." Carlos sighed deeply, his shoulders sagging. "How can I live with myself knowing that? How do I go on?" He turned and looked at Ivan intently.

While listening to his friend, Ivan was becoming increasingly concerned. He was keenly aware that Carlos' love for Hannah had compromised him in the past. Now her illness made him vulnerable to further danger. Ivan would need to function as the guardrail because of his own fondness for them both.

Ivan placed his arm on his friend's shoulder and softly said, "Carlos, I understand that you're under a tremendous amount of stress. You have to remember what happened last time. You also have to know that you won't be able to do anything this time." Ivan paused. "Carlos, I know this is difficult, but I need to hear you tell me that you understand."

Carlos' jaw clenched, and his face contorted. "Yes, I under-stand!" Carlos said. Then he slammed the table with both hands, his wedding ring reverberating against the metal. A deafening silence fell on the cafeteria as everyone turned to look at them. Oblivious, Carlos stormed out of the room.

With tears obstructing his vision, Carlos drove home. His sweaty palms were slicking the leather steering wheel. Finally giv-ing up, Carlos pulled over on the side of the road and surren-dered to his grief. He sat in his car and sobbed, mucous run-ning down his face.

Since Carlos had been orphaned at a young age, his *abueli-ta* had given him unconditional love and support; she was the only family he'd had for many years. After her death, he'd felt utterly alone. When Carlos met Hannah, he felt he was part of a family again; they had built a life together. Now, Carlos was on the verge of losing it all again.

Thrusting his fists in the air, he pumped them furiously at the heavens and shouted "Why?" repeatedly until he was hoarse. Having Hannah in his life had changed everything for him; she'd changed who he was fundamentally; he was not nor would ever be the same Carlos he'd been before he met her. *What will I be after she is no longer?* He was not prepared for that answer. After a while, Carlos cleaned himself up, pulled him-self together, and drove home to help his teenage daughter care for his ailing wife.

3

Assther had developed her own daily routine. After returning home from school, she checked on her mother, who was usual-ly in her room resting. Occasionally, Assther would bake gin-gersnap cookies and bring up some chamomile tea, which they would share together. Sometimes they would play a card game or watch television, or Assther would read her mother a story.

Other times, Assther would curl up next to her mother while she slept, just to be close.

Recently during lunchtime in school, Assther had finally shared with her best friend, Jane, about her mother's illness. Silently, Jane had reached over and had taken Assther's hand. That was exactly what Assther wanted and needed.

The pair sat together holding hands throughout the lunch period, chatting as usual. Assther asked Jane not to share her secret; Assther didn't want the other kids to treat her differently or feel sorry for her. Being a teenager was difficult enough without having to tolerate the sympathetic stares or whispers in the school hallways. Even though Assther understood nothing would ever be normal again, she tried to maintain a semblance of her previous life.

As a child, Assther had felt happy and safe snuggling on her parents' canopy bed. It was plush and large with an oversized comforter and voluminous pillows. Assther loved the cinnamon-colored walls and deep maroon, gathered curtains with matching bedspread. She and her mother used to make the canopy bed into a tent and spent hours playing, reading, and telling stories.

Recalling those events would make the reality of her mother's illness more profound, and Assther desperately missed her mother's vitality and energy. She prayed for her mother's speedy recovery and was terrified of the prospect that she might not.

Hannah's fragrance, a mixture of jasmine and her baking, permeated the room; Assther loved the scent. Recently, Assther had noticed that the smell had changed; she wasn't sure if it was caused by the chemotherapy or her illness. Lying with her mother now felt different—lonelier. Assther wiped her tears, checked on her sleeping mother once more, and went to her room to do her homework.

Chapter 11

1

As time progressed, Hannah began having increased difficulty. She'd tolerated the surgery well enough, but soon began to develop hot flashes and night sweats, which caused her significant insomnia. Hannah was grateful that her abdominal pain had improved, but once she started chemotherapy, she became debilitated, thinner, and unable to do the things she'd been able to do in the past.

Always impeccably clean and well dressed, Hannah found she was unable to wash or dress without assistance. It pained her to have her daughter and husband clean her after one of her explosive bouts of diarrhea or vomiting caused by the chemotherapy. Most days, the marital bed, which had given her and Carlos so much pleasure, now became her prison. A prison from where she remembered the simple pleasures of taking a walk with her family, baking with Assther, volunteering at the food bank of the synagogue, and going out to a restaurant with family and friends.

Most importantly, her precious family, which she'd cultivated and nurtured so lovingly all these years, was wilting before her eyes. Hannah felt and saw her beloved's nightly struggles with sleep, his appetite waning, his posture drooping, and the light dimming in his bright blue eyes. Also, her beautiful daughter was struggling to maintain a normal life, be a teenager and still come home to take care of her. Hannah had spoken with the social workers to support her family. She hoped her condition would improve in the near future.

A few months later, Hannah had an inkling that something was wrong when her old pain returned. She didn't want to mention it to her family. Perhaps because she didn't want to admit it to herself or because she didn't want to worry them. It was time for her appointment with Dr. Rajah, and she and Carlos were driving in the car. Both were quiet for most of the car ride. Out of the corner of her eye, Hannah noticed that Carlos' knuckles were turning white from gripping the steering wheel.

Hannah reached over and grasped his hand and said, "It'll be okay, Ricky."

"I know, Lucy," he replied with a weak smile.

Hannah turned and looked out the car window. It was an overcast day and dark, angry clouds had gathered; it was getting ready to rain again.

2

After Dr. Rajah entered the examination room, she scrutinized the couple. Carlos sat in the chair looking straight ahead, and Hannah was unusually calm.

"How are you feeling, Hannah?" Dr. Rajah asked, studying her patient.

"I'm okay," Hannah replied in a soft voice. She was holding her purse in her lap, avoiding eye contact.

"I have the test results," Dr. Rajah said glancing over at her computer. Turning her attention to the pair, she said in a low tone, "I'm sorry to tell you, but it looks like your cancer has returned."

Jumping out of his chair, Carlos began pacing. Calmly, Hannah sat in the plastic chair.

"What are our options?" Hannah asked, looking up at the doctor. Tears were gathering in her eyes, and she wiped them with the back of her hand.

Dr. Rajah was surprised more by Hannah's reaction than by Carlos'. Over the course of her career, she'd seen patients exhibit this behavior in the past, but it was exceedingly rare. It would appear that Hannah had sensed her cancer had returned and was prepared for the news.

"Well, we can perform surgery again," Dr. Rajah said and watched Hannah for a hint of a reaction. At this point, Carlos stopped pacing, sat down, and turned toward his wife. Hannah's face remained unchanged.

"Or we can start hospice." Silently, Dr. Rajah waited for a response.

Hannah shifted in the chair to reposition herself, grimaced, and exhaled. Carlos swallowed hard, held out his hand, and hoarsely whispered, "Let's go home, honey."

Chapter 12

1

The three of them made the decision together as a family, just as they'd made every decision in the past; they discussed, argued, cried, and prayed. Finally, they made the only decision that made sense given the information, considering the odds of survival and best quality of life for Hannah.

Within a few days, hospice arrived at the house, working with expert precision. The metal hospital bed frame and plastic mattress arrived folded in a V-shape and rumbled over the hardwood floor. Then it settled in the living room. After one of the attendants plugged it in and pushed a button, it sprang to life and unfurled itself. The hospice staff rolled in a wooden side table, oxygen tanks, suction machine, and "supplies," as the nurse explained.

Then the nurse examined Hannah and explained to the family the different services available to them: medical, nursing, social services, non-denominational clergy, and grief services. After answering all their questions, the nurse tucked her patient in her new bed, gave them contact information in a large folder and departed, advising them a nurse would return to see Hannah in the morning. Hannah was admitted to hospice.

The following morning, a nurse appeared at their doorstep and introduced herself as Jemima. She was from the hospice agency and was there to examine Hannah.

"It's this way," Assther said. "My mother's in bed. I'm Assther." As Assther led Jemima to her mother, she was attempting not to stare at the small, plump nurse's incongruous face.

Jemima approached Hannah and said, "Good morning. I'm Jemima. You can call me Jem. I'll be your hospice nurse." She paused. "Whatever you, your husband or daughter need, please don't hesitate to let me know. I'm here to help you. Now, how are you feeling today?"

Jem proceeded to examine Hannah, checked her vital signs, examined her for pressure sores, and asked Hannah and her family if they had any questions.

Three to four times a week, Jem visited Hannah. Sometimes Carlos was home, other times only Assther was present. Occasionally, it was just Jem and Hannah, and Jem would remain after she examined Hannah and read to her, or they would talk. Hannah found sharing her thoughts with Jem was easy; the hesitation that existed when she spoke with Carlos, Assther, or her family did not exist with Jem. Some days, Hannah would allow her emotions free rein, and Jem would sit beside her and hold her hand while she wept.

"Jem," Hannah asked one day, "can I ask you what happened to your face?"

"Several months ago, I had Bell's palsy," Jem said. "Now I look like a pirate." Jem smiled and touched the left side of her face.

"I see. Could you help me sit up?" Hannah asked.

"Sure, Hannah." Jem propped some pillows behind her lower back; Hannah repositioned herself and grimaced, her face distorting, and beads of sweat formed on her forehead.

"Can you pass me a pen and paper?" Hannah asked, pointing to the dresser against the wall. "And roll the table this way?"

"Sure. Anything you need, Hannah," Jem replied.

Jem retrieved a pen and some pink paper from the drawer. Then she rolled the side table for Hannah, positioned it so it was comfortable for her. Leaning forward, Hannah began to write a letter. Before long, her hand began to tremble.

Hannah fell back on the pillows, and with exasperation, she said, "I can't do it!" Tears were streaming down her face.

Gently, Jem took the pen and paper and moved the table away from Hannah. "It's okay, Hannah," she said. "Just tell me what you want to say, and I'll write it down."

2

Several days later, Hannah had an unexpected visitor. It was one of her good days, and she was sitting up in bed, supported by several pillows. The stranger was lanky with very long fingers and wearing a trench coat. Hannah stifled a laugh when she heard his high-pitched voice.

"Hi, Hannah, I'm Dr. Schmeck," he said after he entered the room. "How are you feeling?"

Hannah observed him for several minutes as he looked around the room, rubbing his long hands together like a praying mantis.

"Well, I'm dying of cancer," Hannah said, "so not great." Neither one spoke for several minutes.

"Don't worry," Hannah said. "I don't expect you to say anything." A wry grin formed on her face, and Dr. Schmeck's shoulders relaxed.

Silently, Hannah regarded her guest. "Why are you here now after all these years?" she asked.

"I wanted to reassure you that your family, Carlos and Assther, will be fine." He hesitated. "I'm sure Carlos shared everything with you. We'll take care of them," he said, moving closer to Hannah. "Both Carlos and Assther are part of our family, and we'll do everything in our power to protect them." Hannah directed her gaze to Dr. Schmeck, examining him, probing him with her eyes.

"What does that mean, exactly?"

"It means you don't need to worry about them. No harm will ever come to them." Their eyes locked, and she understood him.

"I believe you, Dr. Schmeck," Hannah said, breaking her gaze and exhaling.

As Dr. Schmeck turned to leave, he heard Hannah say, "Thank you, Dr. Schmeck."

3

Feeling her condition was declining, Hannah knew it was time for her to have an important and difficult conversation with her family. The three of them were together one afternoon, and she said, "Carlos, Assther, I need to talk to you about something."

Since Hannah was unable to bathe, Jem and the hospice aide were sponge bathing and dry shampooing her. Carlos approached his wife and moved the stringy hair from her forehead. Then he perched at the edge of the bed.

"My loves, first I want to thank you both for your love and our life together," Hannah said feebly. She paused to catch her breath and steady her trembling voice.

"You both have made me so happy, and I'm grateful for every minute that I've spent with both of you." Hannah swallowed hard and allowed her tears to fall freely. Assther was seated on the other side of the bed, and Hannah turned to her daughter and said, "Assther, you've been my purpose for living, my light and joy. I want you to always remember that you're loved."

Assther kissed her mother's hand and soft sobs shook her petite frame.

Then Hannah turned to Carlos. "Hannah, please, you don't have to —" Carlos pleaded.

"No, please let me get through this," she interrupted. Carlos put his arms up. Hannah took a deep breath. "I know I don't have to tell you to take care of Assther. You love her as much as I do. I want you to know that you've made me very happy." Hannah bit the corner of her cracked lip, and it began to bleed. "You deserve to be happy, and if you find somebody who makes you happy, I want you to be with that person."

Carlos turned his head away from his wife.

After several minutes, he exhaled deeply and turned back. Then Carlos grasped her hand and lifted it in his. Moving closer to Hannah, Carlos said, "You're as beautiful to me as you were the day we met, the day we were married and every day since. Don't you understand that before I met you, I was all alone?" He swallowed hard, and his voice was choked with emotion. He looked into her eyes as he said, "You made me whole and built us a family. There will never be anybody else for me. I'll love you until the day I die." Tenderly, he kissed her hand, then her forehead.

"I'm tired now," Hanna said weakly. "I need to rest." She turned her head toward the wall. As her family walked away, they heard her sobbing softly.

4

"Come in, Rabbi," Carlos said, as he closed the front door. "Hannah's resting in the living room." Rabbi Tesfaye noticed Carlos looked gaunt with dark circles under his eyes. As Carlos led him through the hallway, the rabbi glanced at family pictures which adorned the walls. *What a beautiful and happy family,* thought the rabbi sorrowfully. They walked in silence to the living room where Hannah's new accommodations were. Each man was absorbed in his own thoughts.

The rabbi considered it his sacred duty to visit congregants when they were ill, and it pained him when he had to visit such a young and vibrant person. Hannah had contributed immensely to the congregation and as a result had become an integral and irreplaceable part of the community.

The rabbi approached Hannah slowly. His experience with the terminally ill informed him that Hannah was declining rapidly. The rabbi sat down and pulled a chair close to her bed, which caused the legs to scrape against the hardwood floor. "Hannah, it's wonderful to see you," the rabbi said. "How are you feeling?"

"I have my good days and my bad days. These days are mostly bad," Hannah replied and extended her hand in his direction. "Thank you for coming, Rabbi."

"It's my pleasure," the rabbi said and stretched out his hand in return. "Is there anything I can do for you or your family?"

Carlos, who was sitting next to the rabbi, jumped up and said, "I'm so sorry, Rabbi. I forgot my manners. Let me get you some tea." He rushed out the room toward the kitchen.

Hannah and the rabbi watched Carlos retreat. There was a long silence before either one spoke.

"Rabbi, do you believe in Karma?" Hannah asked, sighing deeply.

"What do you mean, Hannah?"

"You know, destiny or fate." Hannah's eyes were distant.

The rabbi was accustomed to terminally ill congregants having existential crises; they questioned their actions in life and their eventual afterlife. It was an extremely potent time.

"Forget I said anything, Rabbi. It's okay." Hannah said, meeting the rabbi's gaze.

The rabbi saw tears welling up in her eyes.

"Hannah, as you know in Judaism, there is no heaven or hell. Each of us must live the best lives here while we're alive. Whatever mistakes we make, we should strive to correct them. I've known you for many years, and you are caring and compassionate. You have a beautiful daughter and family, and you should be very proud of that."

The rabbi found his voice breaking as he spoke. He was unsure if his words were having the desired effect.

"Thank you, Rabbi, for your kind words," Hannah said. "Will you promise me that you'll take care of my family after ..." Her voice trailed off, and she remained quiet.

"I promise, Hannah," the rabbi replied and sighed deeply. "Nothing would make me happier."

The rabbi got up and quietly showed himself out.

5

When Assther entered the living room, her mother was in bed. Her eyes were closed. Dressed in a powder blue nightgown, the fleece blanket was pulled up to Hannah's waist. The air was stale. The room had the slight odor of sweat. Mouth open, Hannah's breathing was rapid and shallow. Despite repeated applications of Vaseline by Jem, her lips were cracked. Having lost so much weight, the skin on Hannah's face was sagging and sallow. Her fingers and toes were turning cold and blue. To ease Hannah's discomfort, Jem was administering morphine and oxygen.

Sensing that her mother's death may be imminent, Assther decided it would be best if her father wasn't present during her mother's last moments; he wouldn't be able to handle it. Also, they had already said their goodbyes, and the woman he loved was long gone. It was up to Assther to spare him the anguish. So she suggested they get some dinner together.

That evening, Death entered silently through the window. It had been nearby for months, slowly extracting the life out of Hannah. The curtain moved slightly against the closed window as it entered the room. Sitting by Hannah's bedside, Jem shivered and glanced around her, but saw no one.

Tonight, death hovered over Hannah and observed her for a while. Then its ethereal fingers blanketed her. Face to face with Hannah, Death said, "Hannah, I'm here. It's time to go."

"I'm ready," Hannah replied.

PART II

10 YEARS LATER

Chapter 1

1

In her essays to colleges and medical schools, Assther explained that her mother's battle with ovarian cancer sparked her aspiration to become a doctor. Throughout her mother's struggle with the illness, the doctors, nurses, and other allied health workers had supported the family, decreased her mother's pain, and gave her dignity and control in her final days.

Assther described how she herself wanted to be a part of a healthcare team that provided comfort, alleviated pain, and improved quality of life. Her photographic memory combined with her exceptional academic performance helped Assther gain admittance to UC Berkeley, her parents' alma mater, and eventually to UCSF Medical School.

Every happy occasion would be commemorated at Hannah's gravesite under the boughs of the majestic maple tree. Usually, Assther and her father would bring a picnic basket filled with homemade desserts and champagne. Assther rested her head against the powerful trunk and watch intricately decorated butterflies dart from flower to flower. She'd never shared with her father what the rabbi had told her the day of her mother's funeral. Assther had been immobilized by grief, and the rabbi had approached her while she was standing near her mother's coffin. Sensing Assther's despair, the rabbi had said, "Don't think of it as being the end. Think of it as a transition to another form, just as a caterpillar transforms into a butterfly." Every time Assther noticed the insects' gossamer wings flit in a seemingly random manner, she sensed her mother was nearby.

One summer during medical school, Assther traveled to the Zamora region in rural Mexico and volunteered with a mobile clinic, which visited elderly, pregnant, and incapacitated patients. While working at the clinic, Assther met Ezmy, a fellow volunteer from the University of Oregon; they became fast friends, bonding over the mutual loss of a parent at a young age. Ezmy, who was biracial, wore her hair in a natural afro, and her lithe frame and soft gait belied the heavy weight she carried.

Both fluent in Spanish, the two students eagerly volunteered multiple shifts traveling the long voyages on unpaved and narrow roads to distant villages. The mobile clinic provided much-needed medical care to very appreciative patients. During their shifts, both young women saw the abject poverty and squalor in which these patients lived and were transformed by the gratitude the patients expressed for the care the mobile clinic provided. Their work in Mexico ignited in Assther and Ezmy a passion to help the underserved, which they would continue after they returned home.

After graduation from her residency in family medicine, Assther found a job and began work at a clinic in Oakland – serving mostly Spanish speaking and the underserved population. Her first day of work, she was overjoyed to learn that her friend Ezmy had moved to the Bay Area and was also working at the same clinic – it was a happy reunion.

"Dr. Medina, your first patient is ready," Lizzy, the medical assistant, said.

"Thank you, Lizzy," Assther said, looking up from the computer.

"He's here for piles," Lizzy said. "I left all the supplies you'll be needing for the exam." She had a smirk on her face as she exited the office and made a gesture with her index finger.

"I think you're enjoying yourself too much, Lizzy." Assther smiled.

"Better you than me, Doc," Lizzy responded over her shoulder.

Assther and Ezmy exchanged glances and chuckled.

"Can we have dinner tonight?" Ezmy asked. "I can get a sitter for Suzie."

"I'll be having dinner with my father tonight. How about tomorrow night?"

"It's a date. I better get started too, before the 'Warden' comes around," Ezmy said, stood up from her stool, and walked out of their communal office.

Following close behind, Assther moved down the hallway to the exam room, opened the door, and said, "Mr. Jones, what brings you in today?"

Chapter 2

1

In an effort to stave off melancholy and maintain his mental faculty after retirement, Carlos began to volunteer at the local youth center, mentoring teens in math, computer science, and various languages. Being surrounded by the youthful vitality and helping to unleash their true potential was very gratifying; he saw himself in many of them.

Carlos and Ivan had met regularly over the past several years. One evening, they were having dinner in Carlos' kitchen, and Carlos was explaining this to his friend. Carlos was still living in the same home he had shared with Hannah and the living room where Hannah had spent her dying days had remained unfurnished. Every time Carlos passed the room, the memories were reawakened. Carlos believed it was his penance to pay.

"Some of these kids have great potential, but don't have the self-esteem and support to follow through," Carlos explained with an expression of excitement. The duo had just finished eating sushi from the local Japanese restaurant, and Carlos was clearing the plates and putting the dishes into the sink.

Carlos' appearance remained unchanged, save for a few strands of gray in his otherwise wild brown hair.

"It sounds like you're enjoying the work," Ivan said and gazed up at his friend while resting his hands on his protuberant midsection.

"Yes," Carlos said. "It feels good to see their eyes light up when they understand a difficult concept, or come back and tell me they did well on a test or a project."

Leaning back in the chair, Ivan asked, "How's Assther doing?"

"She's doing great. She's working hard at her new job in a local clinic." Carlos brought a cup coffee for each of them and sat down in his chair.

Taking a sip, Ivan observed a father's pride on Carlos' face. Both men were silent for several minutes.

"Have you been watching the news?" Ivan asked.

"Yes," Carlos replied after a long pause.

"What do you want to do about it?"

"We may have to adjust our plans." Carlos closed his eyes and rubbed them with the palm of his left hand.

Ivan noticed a remote gaze in Carlos' blue eyes. Gently, he touched his friend's arm. "Carlos?"

Carlos's eyes narrowed and he swallowed hard. "You know, it's been almost ten years and it feels just like yesterday that I lost her." His voice was barely audible. "I think about her all the time. I go through my days thinking Hannah would have liked that, I should tell Hannah about this ..." He trailed off.

"Do you know that I visit the gravesite every week. I clear debris or weeds from the headstone and bring fresh flowers. Then I sit on the grass sharing events of my day with her. Sometimes, I finger her name slowly and gaze into her picture embedded into the marble. I tell her amusing anecdotes and the latest news. Other times, I bring a book she would've liked and read chapters out loud."

Carlos paused for several minutes. "I sit for hours listening to Hannah's favorite jazz album." He looked at his friend wistfully and added, "Even now, when I think about her, it hurts to breathe. I still believe that I should've done more." He clenched his jaw.

"Carlos, there was nothing more you could've done."

Carlos turned to his friend and in an even tone said, "I think we both know that's not entirely true."

2

Beeep "Hello, Mr. Medina, this is Tina Ho from the San Francisco Examiner. I'm trying to reach you to talk to you about a story I'm writing regarding surrogate births. I'd really love to get your input on this story. Could you please call me back when you get this message? My number is —."

Standing by his phone, Carlos played the message and quickly deleted it.

"Damn it!"

Carlos' back stiffened, and his hands formed into fists. In the past two weeks, the reporter had called at least half a dozen times trying to reach him. Carlos sighed deeply. He knew the secret wasn't going to be hidden forever; it would eventually be discovered and exposed. Carlos was aware this woman wasn't going to give up; when the phone calls proved futile, the reporter would be visiting him in person.

Carlos had known that the time would arrive when everything he cared about would be in jeopardy; he'd hoped it would never arrive and force him into putting his plan into action. Now, measures needed to be taken to address this complication. Unsure of the exact nature, Carlos was certain that *he* needed to control the outcome at all cost. That was absolutely without question.

Scanning the room, Carlos noticed his wedding picture. His eyes narrowed, and his jaw was fixed with determination. He picked up the phone and dialed.

"Ivan, it's me. We need to meet right away. We have a problem."

Chapter 3

1

Despite the fact that her Chinese-American parents wanted her to become a doctor or a lawyer, Tina Ho had wanted to be an investigative reporter for as long as she could remember. Her passion for journalism had blossomed early in elementary school and was cultivated in college. Initially hired by the San Francisco Examiner to write obituaries, Tina was rapidly promoted to feature stories.

Working with other reporters at the paper, Tina felt an energy in the air while the staff hunted for clues, spoke with sources, and finally wrote stories which illuminated viewpoints, educated readers, and exposed hidden truths. Certainly, there were rivalries, chauvinism, racism, and back-stabbing, but Tina thrived on the competition, and for her, the thrill of the chase of the story was better than anything–even sex.

One January, Tina was assigned to write a story on an art show in the Tenderloin District of San Francisco. The artist was featuring a pastiche of African carvings. While standing near one of the art pieces, Tina had spotted his assistance, Jazmin, and had become immediately captivated. Tina almost neglected to interview the artist.

Three months later, Tina and Jazmin were living together in a small one-bedroom apartment. Jazmin's only condition was that Tina keep her research (which had the map of the United States with different colored pins in different cities, birth certificates and names of corporations) out of sight. Jazmin instantly fell in love with Tina's Rottie-poo, Zeus, that Tina had adopted from the pound, and the trio became an instant family.

Recently, Tina had written and published a series of stories in the Examiner that she'd been investigating for some time. Her reports described children who were characterized as "acting strange" by their parents and were later found to have all been born through surrogates. Across the country there had been multiple accounts in the press.

Several weeks after Tina's story was published, it was picked up by the Associated Press and read by Congressman John Landon from Tennessee, who had aspirations for higher office. The congressman had a personal and longstanding agenda against artificial intelligence and believed it would lead to the destruction of human civilization. After reading Tina's article, Congressman Landon – without any evidence – concluded that these children must be robots. He began participating in morning talk shows proclaiming the need to "protect ourselves and our kids from robots." Quickly, his message went viral and social media was full of incidents of parents panicked that their children were robots. Alarmed parents were bringing their children to their physicians for testing to verify they were human. The congressman had started a mass panic.

After hearing the news about the congressman's claims, Tina returned home distraught. She stood by the door unable to move.

"This is not what I intended when I wrote the story," Tina said. "I never even mentioned anything about robots or artificial intelligence. I don't know where he got his information." Slowly, she moved toward the couch and sat down. Then she buried her face in her hands.

"I know, baby," Jazmin said and sat next to her.

"Did you see what's happening with those parents? Some of them are using this as an excuse to abuse or neglect their kids!" Tina wiped the tears with the back of her hand.

"It's not your fault, Tina."

"Of course it's my fault," Tina said. "If I hadn't written this article, that bastard wouldn't have been able to use it for his soap box!" Tina rushed to the bathroom and slammed the door behind her.

Chapter 4

1

"That smells great," Assther said as she entered the house holding a platter of chocolate chip and almond cookies. A weekly dinner was a tradition for father and daughter, and they met either at the Medina home or at a local restaurant. Carlos had just finished making his signature black beans and rice, to which he usually added pork.

Smiling, Carlos greeted his daughter with a tender kiss on the cheek and Assther began setting the table for two. After they had started eating, Carlos glanced over at his daughter and noticed that her appetite was lacking.

"Mija, how are you?"

"I'm fine, Papi," Assther replied, moving the food around her plate.

"How's work going?" Carlos watched his daughter for several minutes, observing her movement and facial expressions. There was pain on her face and a troubled expression in her eyes. "Mija, what's wrong?"

She sighed. "I'm worried about my friend Ezmy."

"Why are you worried about her?" Carlos asked, leaning forward.

"Ezmy recently moved from Oregon to the Bay Area and is working with me at the same clinic." Assther picked up her wine glass but didn't drink from it.

"That's great. I know you were good friends when you volunteered at the clinic. What's going on with her that's worrying you?" Carlos asked, getting up and refilling his wine glass.

Taking a deep breath, Assther leaned back in her chair and paused; she remembered that day vividly.

Ezmy and Assther had been working ten grueling hours at the mobile clinic in Zamora and were both exhausted but exhilarated after having helped so many needy people. The two of them sat down to a meal of fish tacos and beer. Assther noticed her friend hadn't been herself all day.

"Emzy, are you okay? Is something wrong?"

"Sorry. Yes, I'm fine." Ezmy took a deep breath. "It's just today is the anniversary of my father's death." Tears streaked Ezmy's delicate face.

"I'm sorry, I didn't know," Assther said softly, reaching for her friend's hand.

Ezmy looked up with anguish eyes and asked, "Did I ever tell you how he died?"

Assther shook her head.

Ezmy paused as if reliving the memory once again. After wiping her eyes with the back of her hand, she said, "He had been complaining of headaches for several days, and I was beginning to worry about him because no medication was helping him feel better. After the third day, I begged him to go to the doctor, but he said it would pass, and to give it time. Then suddenly he collapsed in the living room." Ezmy began crying, softly at first then with great heaving sobs.

Assther moved close and placed an arm on her friend's shoulder. "I'm so sorry, Ezmy. It'll be okay," she whispered softly.

Ezmy took a deep breath and blew her nose with a tissue. "Thank you, Assther," she said with a weak smile. Ezmy took a long swig of her beer and folded her legs under her.

"I rushed over to him and tried to wake him up. But I couldn't." Ezmy paused. "I screamed at my mother to call for an ambulance. But she just stood there! Can you believe that?" Ezmy's tears fell silently. "I kept yelling, 'Mom, call an ambulance.'" Ezmy's voice was rising, and her face was contorted.

"Finally, the ambulance came. But it was too late. He was gone ..." Ezmy was trembling. She was silent for several minutes. Assther understood the feeling of grief and loss her friend had experienced.

"He was the only person who loved, understood, and cared about me," Ezmy said in a subdued tone. Her gaze was distant. "After he died, I was all alone in the world. My mother hated my father. She was glad he was dead. She also hated that I reminded her of him."

Assther was surprised to hear these words from her friend. Ezmy was a beautiful person; how could anybody hate her? Assther couldn't understand how any parent could hate their child. *What kind of world do we live in where that is possible?* she thought.

Wrapping her arms around herself, Ezmy shifted in her chair slightly. "I decided I wouldn't eat, wouldn't drink, wouldn't go to school. I felt alone and angry–very angry. Angry at my father for leaving and angry at my mother for being there. There were days I couldn't stop crying." Ezmy breathed deeply. "Then my mother found me in the bathroom just in time and took me to the hospital."

"What happened next?"

"After my short hospitalization, I was started on anti-depressants. I'm still taking them now. As long as I take my medications and see my therapist, I'm okay." There was a prolonged silence.

"Thank you for sharing with me what happened, Ezmy. I'm here for you if you need anything." They embraced tightly as tears streamed down their faces.

While Assther recounted the story to her father, she could still remember Ezmy's courage that day and the bond they had forged after Ezmy had confided in her.

"However ..." Assther paused again, got up, and walked over to the counter to start making Cuban coffee for both of them. "Now Ezmy has a five-year-old daughter, and she just relocated and started this new job." While preparing the coffee, she turned to her father and said, "All these things are stressful enough. Ezmy is a great doctor, really caring, and the patients love her, but our supervisor has been really tough on her."

Assther considered her words for a few minutes and then added, "I don't know how much longer Ezmy can manage the stress. And I don't know how to help her." After the coffee was ready, Assther poured them both a cup. Carlos accepted his and one of Assther's home-made cookies.

Hearing Assther relate Ezmy's story brought Carlos back to Hannah's battle with depression. Recalling how his beloved wife had wasted away from despair, his own helplessness assaulted him like a crashing wave. It pained him that his daughter was going through a similar experience with her friend. Carlos wished he could shelter her from the heartbreak, but he was aware that it was impossible. Instead, he knew he needed to guide her and provide her with the information so she could support her friend.

"Mija," Carlos said, with a sigh, "it sounds like Ezmy doesn't have much of a support system, no family or friends, besides you." He paused and looked intently at his daughter. "You know your mother suffered from depression," he said with a heaviness in his heart.

Assther nodded.

"It's important to make sure Ezmy feels like she is supported." Carlos hesitated. "It's also vital that you know to look for any warning signs."

Assther looked gravely at her father and nodded in agreement.

Chapter 5

1

Meeting at a restaurant that specialized in ribs, Ezmy and Assther found a table at the back for privacy. It was a busy Friday night, and the restaurant was crowded with patrons celebrating the weekend early. The two of them ordered beer, two orders of pork ribs, French fries, and asked for lots of napkins; they expected to make a big mess.

The aroma of their order wafted in their direction before they saw it coming; the sweet/sour smell of the barbecue sauce on the ribs, and the spices on the French fries made them salivate with anticipation. Once the food arrived, they began eating.

Rock-n-roll music was playing in the background, people chatting all around them, and between bites of ribs and fries, Ezmy said, "I'm throwing a 5th birthday party for Suzie in two weeks, and I want you to be there. It's going to be at the park near our house."

"Sure, I'd love to be there. Just let me know the details," Assther said after she finished chewing on her ribs. "How are you and Suzie adjusting to the move?" she asked, taking a bite of a French fry.

"Suzie's doing well in school and making friends. The adjustment has been a little difficult for me," Ezmy said. "You know it takes a while for me to adjust to a new situation, and stress is difficult for me to manage." Ezmy had stopped eating and was wiping her hands on a napkin.

"How are you managing your stress now?" Assther asked, looking up from her food.

Ezmy took a sip of her beer and after a moment replied, "I make sure I don't fall into my old habits, that's one thing." She paused. "And I maintain my routine, which I know is important."

Assther reached over and took her friend's hand, smearing barbeque sauce on it, and said, "You know you can always come and talk to me if you need to. Any time of the day or night."

"I know," Ezmy said. Her face turned slightly warm, and her eyes welled up with tears.

Relocating to the Bay Area had been a difficult decision for Ezmy. When she had discovered that she would be working with Assther, she was overjoyed and knew she'd made the correct decision for herself and Suzie. After her father's death, Ezmy had been alone for so many years. Now, she felt grateful to have Suzie and Assther in her life.

Since losing her father, Ezmy believed there would never be anybody else who would understand, care about, and love her. For the first time in a very long time, Ezmy felt she might actually be happy. Part of her wondered how long it would all last.

2

Several weeks later, Assther was preparing to see her first patient when Ezmy entered the communal office. She had dark circles under her eyes, and her clothes were in disarray. Lizzy, at her heels, entered the room and said, "The computer system is down. We don't know for how long. And patients are waiting for both of you." Finishing her announcement, Lizzy rushed out the door.

Oblivious, Ezmy sat down in her chair and began sobbing. Quickly, Assther closed the door to the office. Then with one hand she offered Ezmy a box of tissues. She picked up the phone with the other hand.

"Hi, Lizzy, this is Dr. Medina. Could you let Dr. Jones' and my patients know we'll be about twenty minutes late? Thank you." Her face grimaced. "Yes, I know that. Just tell them it's because of the computer problems." Assther perched on the chair and furrowed her brow. "Okay, then don't give them any reason. I'm just telling you that we'll need twenty minutes before we can start seeing patients this morning."

Finally Assther hung up the phone. *Take a breath now*, she told herself. *This is bad*. Was this the warning sign her father had warned her about? *What could possibly be wrong?* Assther wondered. She hadn't heard of any issues regarding Ezmy at work. Did this mean it had something to do with Ezmy's personal life? Why wasn't Ezmy confiding in her?

Blowing her nose on the corner of a tissue, Ezmy watched as Assther negotiated a reprieve for them on the phone. She was so grateful to Assther for her friendship, support, and devotion. Suzie and Assther had become the family Ezmy had longed for since the her father's untimely death. Ezmy was desperate to divulge to Assther the problems that were causing her increased stress in the past several weeks. She was, however, ambivalent about how safe it would be for Assther. Ezmy didn't want to involve Assther if there was any chance that it would endanger her in any way. She straightened herself up and took a deep breath. Drawing upon the strength she'd first developed at a very young age, Ezmy steeled herself and reached a decision.

By the time Assther finished her phone conversation, Ezmy had collected herself and was drying her face with the tissues. After hanging up the phone, Assther rolled an office chair next to her friend. Gingerly, she began picking at rogue pieces of chalky tissue that were scattered on Ezmy's face.

"Please tell me what's is going on," Assther said, concern etched on her face. "I can't help you if I don't know what's going on."

"I'm sorry. I didn't mean to scare you. I just haven't been sleeping well in the past few days," replied Ezmy, wringing the tissue with her hands.

"Do you want to go home and get some rest? I can cover for you for the rest of the day," Assther asked.

"No!" exclaimed Ezmy.

Assther flinched. *What's going on? Why doesn't she want to go home?*

"Okay, Ezmy, you really need to tell me what's going on. You know I'm here for you," Assther said, her rising voice matching the panic she was feeling.

Ezmy looked around the room and asked, "Can we talk later today?"

Assther mimed her movement and replied, "Sure. How about after work?" Assther paused and sighed deeply, feeling very concerned about her friend. *Shit, she's becoming paranoid now,* Assther thought.

"But first, let's fix you up. We can't have you looking worse than the sick patients who come to see you, can we?" Assther gave her a wink and pulled out concealer from her makeup bag. Then she began to apply it to Ezmy's face.

Chapter 6

1

Listening to the radio while driving to work, Tina's editor heard the breaking news: Congressman Landon would be considering legislation regarding robotic children, the newscaster reported. The editor reached for the knob and abruptly shut off the radio. His mind drifted back to the meeting he'd had the night before with a mysterious man wearing a bespoke pinstriped suite. The man had instructed him to stop Tina from continuing to investigate the story she was currently working on. Then the mysterious stranger provided him with a press release to print in the next edition of the paper.

The editor wasn't sure he liked being told how to do his job, but years of experience had taught him that there are certain people you don't contradict. The suited man, whom the editor dubbed 'Dapper Dan,' explained it was in everybody's interest that the story die.

Although he understood what needed to be done, he dreaded the task ahead of him. He realized it would be difficult to pry the story from Tina's hands; she'd been working on it for a long time and she was personally invested. The editor liked Tina and respected her and the work she produced. However, there were far-reaching and more powerful forces at work. It was beyond his control.

Meanwhile, Tina woke up that morning having a better perspective and thankful for Jazzy's support. Ready to tackle the day's work ahead, Tina walked into her small cubicle and turned on her computer. While Tina was preparing to start working on her story, her editor's assistant entered and summoned her to his office.

I wonder what's going on, Tina thought. She'd heard the news on her drive to work and wondered if this meeting was related.

Briskly, Tina walked behind the assistant into the editor's over-sized office. Instantly, she noticed something was amiss. Usually, the editor was seated behind his oversized mahogany desk, lean-ing back in his leather chair with his legs crossed in front of him. He liked to smoke a large cigar and issue orders to his staff.

On this particular day, the editor was seated ramrod straight. His eyes, behind his wire-rimmed glasses, bounced from Tina to a suited figure seated in a chair in the corner of the office.

The editor cleared his throat and began, "Please come in, Tina. I'll get right to it. You must've heard about what's going on re-garding the story you wrote."

Standing close to the door, Tina nodded tentatively, unsure what her editor was about to say.

"It's a real shit storm," he said, fidgeting in his leather chair.

Why is he so nervous? She glanced over at the figure in the corner of the office. *Who is this guy?*

The editor blinked several times and took a breath. "I'm sor-ry, but we won't be running any follow-ups to your story." He glanced over at the figure in the corner. Tina thought she no-ticed the figure's head move imperceptibly.

"Wait, what? Why?" She gaped at her editor. "Who is this guy?" Tina said, turning her attention to the mysterious figure.

"Don't worry about him. He's from corporate," the editor re-plied. "I also don't want you doing any more investigating into this story. It's over," he added with finality.

"What are you talking about?" Tina said, her eyes narrow-ing and her shoulder becoming rigid. She felt as if she had been kicked in the stomach. She could feel her blood pressure rising and her ears getting hot.

"Tina," her editor said, leaning forward, "the CDC and HHS will be issuing a joint press release today that all those children you wrote about were infected by a virus and they were not ro-bots. The virus has been contained and the threat has been neu-tralized." He handed her the press release.

After taking the sheet of paper, Tina said, "But it's not true!" She clenched her fists, crumbling the paper. "My articles don't mention anything about robots."

The editor put up his hands.

"That's the story we will be printing," he said. "And I need you to promise that you'll stop investigating this whole thing because there is nothing to investigate. Do you understand?" He waited for a response.

Tina was immobilized with shock and disbelief.

Her editor fixed his gaze on her and repeated, "Tina, I need to hear you say it."

Steeling herself, Tina took several deep breaths and finally said, "Yes. I got it!" Marshalling all her powers to keep her tears at bay, she dashed out of the office, catching one last glimpse of the shadowy figure.

2

For the second night in a row, Tina returned home in distress and found Jazmin waiting to ease her discomfort. After Tina recounted the events of her meeting with her editor, Jazmin kissed her and said, "Come to bed, baby. Jazzy will make it all better." She took Tina's hand and guided her to their bedroom. Tina looked at Jazzy's beautiful toffee complexion and gap-tooth smile and accepted her hand.

Lying in bed enveloped in Jazzy's warm embrace, Tina was able to block out the world and feel the love and acceptance she was freely given. But that would only be temporary. Unable to sleep, Tina disentangled herself from Jazzy's arms and walked over to her desk.

As Tina flipped open her computer, her thoughts were racing. After all this time and the work she'd invested, how could she stop now? She opened a private browser, turned on her VPN, and began typing. Suddenly, her editor's warnings replayed in her head, and she saw the shadowy figure in the corner of his office. *Who was that fucker? If this is a government cover-up, they can track me even on a private browser and VPN!* She looked behind her at Jazzy's sleeping form. *No, I've already lost too much. I can't risk losing any more.* Slowly, Tina closed her computer.

Chapter 7

1

After they had finished their workday, Ezmy and Assther sat together at a coffee shop close to work. Assther noticed that Ezmy was drinking herbal tea and eating a chocolate brownie. Assther knew Ezmy ate chocolate whenever she was stressed.

"How was your day?" Ezmy asked, taking a sip of her tea.

"Not great," Assther said with a frown. "I saw a thirty-year-old patient with a breast mass who probably has breast cancer. She's from Guatemala, has three kids and no support system here." She took a bite of a raspberry muffin.

"I'm sorry, that is a bad situation. Hopefully the social worker can help the patient."

"Yes, if we can get her evaluated and tested in time. My fear is that she'll fall between the cracks, and then come back a year or two from now with more advanced disease. That'll be a real tragedy." Assther stared out the window with a troubled expression.

"This case must be difficult for you, Assther," Ezmy said.

"Yes. It is." Assther was silent for several minutes. "This was one of the reasons I became a doctor. I wanted to help save lives and help prevent people from dying from cancer."

Assther chewed the corner of her lip and leaned back in her chair. "I was just thinking about Mrs. Gonzalez," Assther said with a faint smile. "Do you remember her?"

"How could I forget? That was our first experience as medical students together." Ezmy laughed out loud. "I'll never forget that bloodcurdling scream you let out, Assther."

Assther cocked her head to the side and smiled. "It would've been interesting to see how you'd have reacted in the same situation."

"Probably the same way," Ezmy replied, laughing.

"That incident was one of the reasons I didn't go into OB/GYN," Ezmy said.

"Do you remember her four children?"

"Of course. *I* was the one taking care of them," Ezmy said.

Early in their training, Assther and Ezmy had been assigned to examine Mrs. Gonzalez, for whom the birth of her fifth child was imminent. They were both working with a mobile clinic in Zamora, Mexico. While Assther was examining Mrs. Gonzalez, Ezmy was trying to entertain the four children by telling them stories and doing arts and crafts.

Assther began her evaluation of Mrs. Gonzalez by measuring her blood pressure, pulse, fundal height, and listening for the baby's heart rate. Then she examined Mrs. Gonzalez. "How are you feeling?" Assther asked her patient.

"Tired," was the reply with a heavy sigh. "I've been having some heartburn and trouble sleeping because the baby is very active at night." Mrs. Gonzalez gave a gap-toothed smile and patted her gravid abdomen.

"Do you have any help now? Will you have any when the baby arrives?" Assther asked.

"Yes," replied Mrs. Gonzalez. "My husband isn't here, but I have family and friends who'll help with the baby and the kids."

"I have to use the bathroom *now*," Mrs. Gonzalez exclaimed. She heaved herself awkwardly from the chair. Assther followed her patient and waited outside the bathroom door.

"Help! Help!" Mrs. Gonzalez shrieked from the bathroom.

Quickly Assther opened the door. "What's wrong, Mrs. Gonzalez?"

"The baby is coming!"

To Assther's surprise, she saw the baby's head protruding from between Mrs. Gonzalez's legs. Assther felt a surge of anxiety and was unsure what to do next. She took few deep breaths and felt her body relax.

"It's okay, Mrs. Gonzalez. Let's just walk back to the bedroom, and you can lie down. Then we'll get the doctor right away."

Gently, Assther guided Mrs. Gonzalez back to her bedroom and helped her into bed. Having settled Mrs. Gonzalez, she cried, "Ezmy, the baby's coming! Get the doctor! The baby's coming. Get the doctor!"

"Dr. Gomez told us he was very proud of the way we handled ourselves," Assther said.

"Yes. It was definitely an interesting experience. I also remember being very grateful that you were there, Assther," Ezmy said, reaching over to grasp her friend's hand.

"The feeling is mutual, you know that." Assther smiled. "Now, it's your turn on the hot seat. What's going on with you?"

Ezmy's body stiffened and she shifted in her chair as she surveyed the coffee shop.

"I had a meeting with 'the Warden' a few days ago. She told me my performance review was below average and that there had been some complaints. If I don't change my 'attitude' they will be letting me go." Ezmy's voice was low and subdued, and her expression was one of resignation.

"Did you talk to her about your concerns regarding the workload, computers, hygiene issues and all that?"

"Yes." Ezmy began playing with stray pieces of food on the table. "I talked to her about that, but she wasn't interested."

"What are you going to do?"

"I don't know." Ezmy's gaze was downcast, and her shoulders were sagging.

"Ezmy, I'm worried about you," Assther said, moving her chair closer. "How are you dealing with all this stress?" She leaned forward after readjusting herself in her chair.

"I'm doing everything I know how to do!"

"Is there anything else that's going on that's adding to your stress?" Assther asked, looking at her friend. *Like why don't you want to go home?*

Measuring her words carefully, Ezmy replied, "No, there's nothing else." Her eyes shifted away to avoid Assther's gaze.

Feeling increasingly uneasy, Assther reached out and grasped her friend's hands. Taking a deep breath, she said, "Ezmy, you're my dear friend, and I love you." She hesitated. "I'll do anything to make sure you're safe and happy. Please tell me how to help you." *How can I help my friend when she's shutting me out?*

"Thank you. I appreciate that," Ezmy said, meeting Assther's gaze. "There's nothing you can do. Everything'll be fine."

2

Having been profoundly close to her father, his death had affected Ezmy significantly. For many years after his passing, she believed she was unworthy of being loved. Ezmy could still recall his soft hands, his gentle nature, and his contagious laugh. She cherished the brief time they'd spent together.

Ezmy's memories of her father were the source for her resilience. Through years of counseling and treatment, her self-worth grew and was bolstered when she met and befriended Assther. Also, having Suzie in her life had been a miracle. Assther and Suzie became Ezmy's new family.

Ezmy had been particularly grateful for Assther's response when she revealed to her about her suicide attempt after her father's death. It had strengthened their friendship.

Now that Ezmy had the family she'd always wanted, she didn't want to lose everything. Ezmy loved her work, and thanks to Suzie and Assther, her mood had improved. However, Ezmy was beginning to question if she'd somehow defied the laws of nature. Perhaps her happiness would be short lived. Ezmy's thoughts of worthlessness began to resurface with increasing frequency, and she struggled to drive them away.

Frequently Assther observed Ezmy during their interactions and concluded that her friend was improving. Ezmy was looking less stressed and smiled more. Delighted that her friend's low spirits had lifted, Assther hoped that whatever stress she was experiencing at home had resolved. Assther had noticed a significant improvement as she watched Ezmy interact with the staff, patients, and the 'Warden.'

The two of them enjoyed evenings together having dinner or coffee after work. Ezmy shared stories of Suzie, or her patients or an upcoming vacation she was planning. Assther was happy with the positive signs she observed.

After the incident, Assther would analyze, scrutinize, and dissect every word, action and inaction. There would be sleepless nights looking for patterns in behavior that may have been there that she should've predicted in her friend or should've discovered that may have changed events. Assther would turn over in her mind whether she shared any blame for what happened. But at that moment, Assther was content enjoying time with her friend.

As soon as Assther arrived at work, she sensed the mood was different; something was wrong. Looking around the hallways, she heard low murmurs and observed some people weeping. Others' heads were hung low. *What's going on?* she thought as she entered the office she shared with Ezmy. *Where is Ezmy? She should be here by now.*

Suddenly, Assther had a feeling of impending doom. Several minutes later, the 'Warden' entered in the room and shut the door. Her elderly face was deeply creased.

NO! Something shrieked inside Assther, *NO! DON'T TELL ME! I DON'T WANT TO KNOW!*

"Assther, please sit down," the 'Warden' said with a grave expression. She folded her arms over her pendulous breasts and stood by the desk.

"No, I don't want to sit," Assther said, standing by the door. She wrapped her arms around herself.

"Please sit down, Assther."

"Just tell me what happened. Is it Ezmy? Oh God, it's Ezmy, isn't it? Please don't tell me it's Ezmy." Assther slid into a chair, unable to support her weight.

"Assther," said the 'Warden,' "Ezmy is gone." She sighed heavily with downcast eyes.

Assther heard herself howl, and she brought her hands to her mouth. "This can't be. This can't be," she wailed repeatedly, rocking back and forth. It was as if the earth fell away from under her. Assther was unable to hear or feel anything for several minutes. Her skin was numb, and her ears were ringing. She sat in the chair attempting to process what she had just been told.

"What happened?" Assther whispered. "I just talked to her yesterday and she was fine!" Assther did not know what to do with herself. She didn't know where to go to decrease the pain she was feeling.

"Apparently her daughter found her in the bathroom. She went to the neighbor to get help." There was a long pause. "By the time the ambulance arrived, it was too late," the 'Warden' said. She hesitated for several minutes, looked at Assther and added, "I'm very sorry, Assther."

"Sorry?!" Assther said. Her face was contorted.

"We're closing the clinic for the day. We'll be having some therapists available for counseling." As she exited the office, the 'Warden' added, "Please let me know if there's anything I can do to help."

Assther remained alone in the office she shared with her friend. How was this possible? Ezmy was like a sister to her. Although Assther didn't have any siblings, she loved Ezmy, and through the years the two had become a family. Now, Assther had lost another member of her family, and her thoughts drifted to her mother's death. Then Assther replayed in her mind all the experiences she had shared with Ezmy. A deep abyss was developing in her, and Assther cupped her face in her hands and wept.

Chapter 8

1

Attending a parent's funeral as a child has a lasting effect; being at Ezmy's funeral was somehow much more difficult for Assther. The church was filled to capacity for the funeral service as the friends and family sat in the wooden pews and others stood in the back. The air was thick with grief as the mourners conversed in subdued tones. A large screen was located by the dais showing a video montage of Ezmy's brief life.

During the service, people described Ezmy's gentle character and loving heart. Former patients, often becoming emotional, described how Ezmy would "talk to them," "listen to them," make them feel important, and even saved their lives from life-threatening diseases. Listening to the emotional speeches, Assther was unsure if she'd be able to endure the entire service. The loss and anguish she felt was overwhelming.

After the funeral finished, a woman who looked familiar approached Assther. She had fine blond hair and was wearing a dress that accentuated her voluminous breasts.

"You must be Assther," the woman said, extending her hand.

"Yes, that's right. Do I know you?".

"I'm Cheryl. Ezmy's mother," she said with a thin smile.

Assther remembered a picture of the woman in Ezmy's apartment.

"Nice to meet you. I'm sorry for your loss," Assther said and extended her hand.

"Thank you." Cheryl paused for several minutes. "You probably know my daughter and I weren't very close." She bit her lip. "In fact, we hadn't talked for five or six years. But I received a letter from her two weeks ago, and she told me that you were a good friend to her." Assther watched the woman struggle to maintain her composure, a battle she was losing.

"I'm glad she found someone she felt she could lean on and trust. We never could get on the same page no matter how hard I tried. After my husband died, I lost them both." Cheryl ran her chubby fingers under her eyes, smoothed her makeup, and sighed. She swallowed hard and tossed her head back. Then, reaching out, Cheryl pulled Assther into her arms.

"Thank you for being there for my baby." Cheryl released Assther and added, "I know she loved you, and you loved her too. I'll always be grateful to you for that." Then Assther watched Cheryl walk away.

While trying to process the encounter with Ezmy's mother, Assther thought she saw two suited men watching her; when she turned her head, they'd vanished.

2

Having been told she needed to see an attorney regarding Ezmy, Assther drove to the office of Jonas Johansen Esq., whose office was located in a converted row house in Oakland. Assther entered the the office into what must've originally been the foyer. Against the wall with peeling wallpaper, there was a wooden desk with stacks of paper in disarray. A folding chair rested against the desk. After stopping briefly and looking around, Assther followed the signs down a hallway into one of the rooms at the back of the house. Faded outlines of picture frames lined the walls.

Mr. Johansen had been expecting her and was sitting in his chair waiting. The wall closest to the attorney was covered floor to ceiling with law books, heaped in a massive stack in the corner. The desk was positioned in the far end of the crammed and overcrowded room. The floor had green shag carpeting–undoubtedly from the original owner – and there was a faint odor of Old Spice in the air.

The attorney himself was a heavyset African American man in his seventies, almost completely bald except for a tuft of hair in the very front of his head. Having lost weight recently (due to some health problems), he had ill-fitting dentures despite the use of denture adhesive. This caused him to lisp when he spoke.

"Please come in, Ms. Medina," he said. "Please have a seat." He pointed to a chair in front of his desk.

"Thank you, Mr. Johansen." After settling into the seat, Assther took a breath. "Why am I here?"

"Ms. Jones wanted me to talk with you in the event of her death." He shifted his massive weight in his oversized chair, which caused the leather to squeak. "First, I'd like to express my condolences."

"Thank you," Assther said.

Assther struggled to understand the man and moved her chair closer to the desk.

"Ms. Jones cared deeply for you. That's why she wanted you to take care of Suzie," he said, opening a file on his desk.

"What?" replied Assther, leaning forward. "I don't understand."

"Her daughter, Suzie. She wanted you to take care of her," the attorney repeated, flipping through some papers.

I can't take care of Suzie. I'm not ready to be a mother. "What about Ezmy's family?" After several minutes of reflection, Assther added, "Is this what Ezmy really wanted?"

"Yes," said the attorney. "She wrote you a letter. It's all in here." He handed Assther a manila envelope.

"Won't Ezmy's family want to take Suzie?" Assther asked, remembering her meeting with Cheryl.

"Ms. Jones didn't think so." The attorney was rifling through his desk searching for something. "But if you have any problems, just call me and I'll be glad to help you." He offered Assther his card.

For several moments, Assther sat in the chair and tried to understand what she had just been told and how her life would be changed once again. Assther knew she had to care for Suzie because her beloved friend wished her to do it. Her friend trusted her enough to entrust her most precious procession to her. Assther was going to honor that obligation.

"Thank you, Mr. Johansen," Assther said and stood to leave.

Assther watched the attorney struggle to rise from his chair, once, twice, thrice, then succeed.

"You're welcome, Ms. Medina," he said with a smile. As soon as she exited his office, he dropped like a stone into his oversized chair.

Chapter 9

1

After settling Suzie in bed, Assther poured herself a glass of white wine and sat on her couch to look through the manila envelope. She had to admit she was uneasy about what she might discover. What would the contents of the envelope reveal? What was her friend hiding all those months that she didn't feel comfortable or perhaps safe to share?

In her current emotional state, Assther was unsure she was prepared to cope with the secrets that were hidden inside the envelope. Ezmy's lawyer had said that her dear friend had written her a letter. Assther felt anger growing inside her. *Why would Ezmy write me a letter instead of talking to me? All those times I begged and pleaded with her to tell me what was wrong; instead of telling me the truth, she wrote a letter? Didn't she know I would've done anything to help her? Why didn't she feel she could've trusted me with whatever she was going through?*

The next instant, Assther was overtaken by guilt for her anger. *Maybe Ezmy had her reasons for what she did? Maybe she wanted to protect me?* At this moment, she had upturned the manila envelope and the letter slid out and hit the coffee table with a thump.

Assther felt a familiar feeling she couldn't identify. Suddenly, she felt a wave of memories and emotions that hurled her back to the time she'd read her mother's letter many years before. She was unable to navigate the emotions she was experiencing.

"I can't do this today!" Nearly knocking over the wine glass, Assther rushed to the bathroom. No longer able to suppress her emotions, she sat on the toilet and wept.

The following morning, Assther woke up on the couch and found Suzie standing motionless by the coffee table. The child was staring at her. Yawning and stretching, Assther tried to get some circulation to her stiffened joints. She hadn't slept well. Her head was throbbing. For several minutes after she woke up, Assther had forgotten about losing her dear friend and what she'd asked her to do. Then all at once, the events of the past several days hit her. She sat upright and cradled her head.

"Good morning, Suzie. Are you hungry? Would you like some breakfast?" Assther asked.

No reply.

"Suzie, would you like a warm breakfast or cold cereal this morning?" Assther repeated, rising to a seated position and looking at Suzie. Suzie remained silent and motionless by the coffee table. *Okay,* thought Assther, *maybe that's her way of grieving.*

Assther led the girl toward the television, chose the local PBS station, and sat her down on the carpeted floor.

"You like this show, right? I'll bring you some Cheerios to nibble on."

Mutely Suzie glanced up at Assther.

I'm not a parent and I see children at work all the time, but I don't think this is normal, thought Assther. The aroma of the Cheerios made Assther hungry, so she poured herself a bowl and took it to the coffee table.

Here we go, she told herself and drew a deep breath. Assther lifted the letter and opened it gingerly. Ezmy's beautiful cursive was on the envelope. Assther had always envied her friend's penmanship. Then Assther began to read.

Dear Assther,
First, I want to thank you for your love and friendship throughout the years we've known each other. Ever since my father died, I never thought I would ever find another person who would love me, respect me and become my family. I never thought I would ever have a family like you and Suzie. It was so much more than I ever thought I deserved...

Assther stopped reading for a moment, unable to continue. *Was it too early for a glass of wine?* Ezmy's face flashed in her mind: her beautiful light brown eyes, the way her lip curved up when she smiled. Assther cared deeply for Ezmy, and she felt despair knowing that Ezmy felt she didn't deserve to be loved.

Steeling herself again, Assther restarted reading.

You've been a very important part of my life and I'll always be grateful.
I want to apologize about the way things happened. Please don't blame
yourself. You're the best friend I could've had, and I couldn't have got-
ten through many of the difficulties I've had without your care and sup-
port. There was nothing you could've done to change things.
I've one final favor to ask of you. You're the only person that I can trust
who'll be able to take care of my Suzie. The only one who'll make sure
that she'll be safe. Nobody else can do that. Please, promise that nothing'll
happen to my daughter and that you'll do everything to keep her safe.
I love you with all my heart. I'm deeply sorry for the pain that I've
caused you. Please, know things had become too overwhelming and I
had no choice.
All my love always,
Ezmy

With tears in her eyes, Assther took the letter and kissed it.
She glanced over at Suzie and didn't understand what danger
Ezmy felt she was in. *Does this explain why Ezmy didn't want to*
go home? Not quite. There's something I'm missing, and it had some-
thing to do with Suzie.

Assther poured out the rest of the papers from the manila
folder on the coffee table and examined them. *Holy shit! This*
doesn't make any sense. She found Suzie's birth certificate. The
mother was not Ezmy. It was Victoria McPherson. *Who the hell is*
Victoria McPherson? Assther examined the place of birth: Boston,
Massachusetts. *What's going on here?*

2

Early the following morning, Assther decided to go to Ezmy's
apartment. Suzie needed additional clothes, and it would be
an opportunity for Assther to get more information. As soon
as she entered the apartment, the memories she'd shared with
her beloved friend washed over her. The fading traces of the
Mademoiselle perfume that Ezmy wore still permeated the air.

Assther walked around the apartment and glanced at the pictures on the bookshelf. She kissed them tenderly with her fingertips. Then she touched the hardwood table where they regularly ate dinner and brushed her fingers over the leather couch where they watched movies.

After Assther gathered some supplies for Suzie, she began her investigation. An hour later, Assther discovered a contract Ezmy had signed with a surrogate agency in Boston. The paperwork was hidden in a drawer in Ezmy's desk. *Could this have something to do with Suzie?*

Ezmy's calendar contained a notation for a meeting with someone named Tina Ho. A newspaper clipping was attached: *Nationwide Reports by Parents of Children Acting Strange Linked to A Boston Surrogate Agency*: by Tina Ho. Assther was unsure how this surrogate agency was connected to Ezmy's strange behavior and eventual suicide. Assther knew what her next step would be; it was necessary for her to talk with Tina Ho.

3

While preparing for her meeting with Assther, Tina discovered she was Carlos Medina's daughter. Tina would definitely use that fact to her advantage and get the information she needed. It would be a sort of quid-pro-quo.

The two met at the Peet's Coffee Shop on Piedmont Avenue on an overcast afternoon. They had pre-arranged to sit at the back of the shop. Tina brought Zeus along and tied his leash loosely to a pole outside the café. She was already seated at a table when Assther entered the coffee shop.

As Assther entered the coffee shop, she detected the odor of coffee which pervaded the air and had the tendency to cling to her clothing. The establishment was crowded with patrons, and jazz music was just barely audible over the ambient noise. As Assther navigated to the corner table where Tina was seated, she passed an elderly couple sharing a pastry, a gentleman in a heated discussion gesticulating wildly, and a wailing infant whose mother appeared completely exhausted.

"I'm Assther. You must be Tina Ho, the reporter." Assther extended her hand. Taking a seat with her coffee, Assther noticed that Tina had multiple piercings in her eyebrows and one in her nose. *Not what I would've imagined a reporter would look like, but to each her own,* thought Assther.

"Yes, I'm Tina. It's nice to meet you." Tina introduced herself, extending her tattooed hand. "I'm sorry for your loss, Assther."

"Thank you," replied Assther, attempting to keep her expression neutral. She was weary of the condolences. Assther wished people would finally stop telling her they were sorry. They didn't kill Ezmy; why were they sorry? On the other hand, she realized if they didn't say anything, that would be equally upsetting.

4

"I wanted to meet with you because you had a meeting with my friend, Ezmy," Assther said. "I understand that you two had discussed your story regarding the children acting strange." Assther took a sip of her coffee.

"That's right," Tina said. "I met Ezmy last month after she'd read my article in the paper. She wanted more information."

"Yes," Assther said. "I saw a clip of your article in her calendar." She placed her cup on the table and met Tina's gaze. "What exactly did Ezmy want to know?"

Tina regarded Assther for a short while. "Well, it goes back years ago when Ezmy had been unable to have kids," Tina said, leaning in. "About six years ago, Ezmy used a surrogate program."

Assther nodded. "I found a contract for the program in her apartment. The program was based in Boston."

"That's right." Tina was rotating her coffee cup in a circular manner. "Well, Ezmy had Suzie through the program." Tina

107

paused again and took a sip of her coffee. "If you read my article, you would know it's about kids who went through the same surrogate program and since then have started acting strangely." Tina began playing with her coffee cup again.

Assther leaned back in her chair and scrutinized Tina, trying to understand what she was saying. Glancing around the shop, Assther observed other patrons enjoying their drinks, engaged in animated conversations, or working on their computers. Were they aware of the secrets that were being revealed to her today? A part of Assther wished she was one of them, living in blissful ignorance.

After several minutes of reflection, Assther turned her attention to Tina and asked, "Are you telling me Suzie had been acting strange?" *Maybe this explained some of Ezmy's behavior,* thought Assther.

"Apparently," Tina said. "According to Ezmy, Suzie would stand and stare for hours. Sometimes, she would repeat things that Ezmy would say back to her. Other times, she was unable to get the child to sleep." Tina rose from her chair and glanced out the window toward the pole.

A large knot formed in Assther's stomach as she remembered the events of the previous day. *This must be why she didn't want to go home. This is what she didn't want to share with me and probably what she wanted to protect me from. Oh Ezmy!*

"What about the press release from the CDC and HHS stating that it was a virus that caused the kids to act abnormally?"

"Ezmy didn't believe it," Tina said, leaning back in her chair. "She told me as a doctor she knew what she was observing in her daughter wasn't caused by an infectious disease. That's why she wanted to meet me."

Assther nodded, putting her finger to her lips in rumination. She realized she was just starting to understand what Ezmy must have been experiencing.

"It seems you've been researching this story for a long time."

"Yes," Tina replied curtly and became quiet. Her eyes shifted downward. "I started investigating this story after the same thing happened to my sister." Tina looked up and met Assther's gaze.

"What do you mean the same thing?"

"My sister, Eloise, couldn't have any kids. She used the same surrogate agency in Boston." Tina's voice was strained, and she cleared her throat. "Eloise had a little boy named Jimmy. She loved her son more than anything else in the world. We all did. When Jimmy turned six years old, he fell asleep and we couldn't wake him up." Tina paused for several minutes and Assther saw tears collected in the corners of her eye.

"We called the ambulance. When they arrived, they said he was dead. Of course, Eloise was distraught." Tina was wringing her hands, and her face was distorted.

"Afterwards, something unusual happened. Some 'government people' came to our house and removed Jimmy in a special van. We were advised we couldn't see him or bury him." Tina paused. "Eloise has never recovered." There was silence between them for several minutes.

Then Tina's voice and demeanor became more controlled. "That was six years ago, and I've been investigating the story ever since."

Assther gaped at Tina in astonishment. It sounded like something out of a science fiction novel or television show: ludicrous, preposterous – and yet something about it rang true.

"So Suzie is like Jimmy?" Assther asked. "Does this mean Suzie will die like Jimmy?" she added with terror gripping her heart.

"I believe Suzie *is* like Jimmy, but I don't know if the same fate awaits her," Tina said.

They both contemplated the information they had been discussing. If what Tina was saying was true, how was Assther going to be able to protect Suzie? How was she going to be able to keep her promise to Ezmy?

Reaching for her coffee cup absentmindedly, Assther asked in a slow and deliberate tone, "What have you found out since your article was published?"

Tina's expression brightened, and she became more animated. "Well, all the children who've been acting strange, whether it is malfunctioning like Suzie or not functioning like Jimmy, their surrogate mothers were one of three women who all worked for the same Boston company." Tina paused for several minutes to gather her thoughts. "Apparently, the company told the would-be parents to provide their egg/sperm samples to be implanted into the surrogate. Part of the contract, which is strictly binding, is no visitation of the surrogate during the pregnancy. The surrogate is said to be kept in a particular clinic in Boston receiving special treatment to optimize the fetus' health. Only video chatting is allowed. Once the nine-month gestation is reached, the couple/parent flies to Boston to pick up the newborn." Tina leaned back with satisfaction.

"How much does the process cost?" asked Assther.

"Fifty thousand dollars," Tina said with a smirk.

"There's more, isn't there?" asked Assther, seeing Tina's hesitant expression.

"Yes," Tina replied, shifting in her seat. "I'm afraid so."

"Well. How much worse can it be?" *Maybe I shouldn't have asked that*, thought Assther, the knot in her stomach tightening.

"Well, my source tells me that a government agency took Jimmy and others like him and has been doing experiments on them," Tina said. "Also, the source believes these infants are humanoid robots that were created by one of your father's co-workers."

Eyes wide, Assther fell back in her seat as though she'd been slapped. *What does my father have to do with this? What's this crazy woman talking about? None of this is making any sense!* The room began to spin, and she felt nauseated.

Assther grabbed her bag and bolted from the café, shoving the door open. Reaching the sidewalk, she released the contents of her stomach.

Rushing after her, Tina found Assther with one arm propped against the wall and a string of saliva dripping from her mouth.

"Are you okay?" Tina asked, offering Assther a napkin.

Assther gave her a withering look and waved her away.

"Assther, I need to talk to your father," Tina said. "I've been trying to get in touch with him, but he won't return my calls." Tina paused for several minutes, surveying the street. "I helped you, Assther. Now you owe me."

Out of the corner of her eye, Assther noticed Zeus, who was loosely leashed to the pole. As soon as the dog saw her, he began to bark and growl.

"Down, Zeus, down," Tina commanded. After rushing to the animal, she grasped the leash with both hands. The dog heaved and pulled at the restraint with all his might. While staring at the dog, Assther marshalled her strength and raced to her car, just barely avoiding the animal.

"Calm down, Zeus," Tina said. "What's wrong with you?" She struggled to calm the distraught animal.

5

After finally putting Suzie to bed, Assther settled on the couch with a glass of wine. She needed to process what Tina had revealed to her earlier that day. Assther tried to reason through the information logically and scientifically, like her training had taught her. If Jimmy had been 'conceived' through a surrogate and began to malfunction and was found to be a humanoid robot, then the same applied to Suzie and all those other children that Tina was investigating. *Oh my God. Annabelle*, Assther realized. She'd forgotten about Annabelle.

Assther and her family were gathered for dinner, and she was recounting her day.

"Today, Annabelle got hit in the head with a ball during recess and it made a sound like this: *boiiing*." Assther giggled. "Then after recess she started acting very funny."

"What do you mean, mija?" her father had asked. He had stopped eating and was looking intently at his seven-year-old daughter.

"Mr. Rosen was asking a question, and Annabelle stood up and was repeating everything Mr. Rosen was saying. First, Tommy started laughing, then the whole class was laughing. Mr. Rosen's face got really red," Assther said with a grin.

Assther noticed that her parents had exchanged glances.

"Then Carla, who's such a cry baby, started crying. Pretty soon everybody was crying. Mr. Rosen took Annabelle out of the room by the arm, and we didn't see her for the rest of the day. She was still repeating the words as she walked out the door." Assther paused and looked at her father. "What do you think is wrong with her? Do you think she'll be okay?"

"I hope so, mija," Carlos said, caressing his daughter's cheek.

Assther watched as her mother abruptly excused herself and left the dinner table. That night, Assther thought she heard the faint sound of her mother crying in the next room, but she wasn't sure.

Years ago, Assther's father had told her she had been conceived using a surrogate; did that make her a humanoid robot? No, she dismissed that notion immediately. All the 'robots' were malfunctioning as children. She was almost thirty. How was her father's colleague involved in all this? Assther felt like she was attempting to assemble a jigsaw puzzle without knowing what the final picture was supposed to be. And all the pieces were the same color.

Looking up, Assther noticed Suzie standing by the kitchen staring at her. Assther didn't know how long Suzie had been standing there – watching her, observing her, recording her? Monitoring her? The knot in her stomach that had formed after her conversation with Tina, shifted to her throat.

Chapter 10

1

After finally calming Zeus down, Tina returned to her apartment. While sitting on the couch and petting the dog, Tina reflected on the encounter with Assther. Assther's reaction didn't surprise her. There was a great deal of information she'd shared with her; Tina just hoped Assther would reciprocate and persuade Carlos Medina to call her. She desperately needed his insight to finish her investigation.

After her meeting with Ezmy, Tina had restarted her research but with a great deal of caution to keep Jazzy–and everyone else–safe. What baffled and gnawed at her was Zeus' reaction to Assther. Even though he was a rescue from the pound, in the three years they'd been together, she'd never seen him react that way. The only other time she'd seen an animal react this way was when Eloise's dog –

Whoosh

A folded piece of paper suddenly appeared under Tina's door. She picked it up and read it.

Meet 11:30, usual place

The note was from her source. Hopefully he had some more information for her about this case. Tina found her source to be somewhat paranoid; he always wanted to meet at night, behind an abandoned restaurant. She'd played along with the cloak and dagger because his information had always been accurate and reliable. It was worth the risk as long as he continued to deliver the information she required.

After eating dinner with Jazzy, at 11 o'clock Tina drove to the location of the meeting. The area was secluded, unlit, and permeated with the stench of urine. Tina kicked an empty beer can out of her way, and it reverberated as it struck the side of the fire hydrant. Walking briskly, Tina held her mace in her right hand as she moved. Sirens wailed in the distance. The lamp posts buzzed overhead. A homeless woman was huddled with her blankets sleeping in a doorway, her cart crammed with her earthly belongings within arm's reach.

Approaching her from behind, Tina's source said, "Hi, Tina."

Quickly Tina pivoted, ready to fire her mace.

"It's me, Tina!" he yelled, holding his hands up defensively.

"Are you crazy?" Tina said. "Don't ever do that. I almost maced you!"

"I'm glad you didn't," he said, "for both our sakes."

"Yeah, okay," Tina said. "Why am I here?" She could still feel her heart pounding against her chest. Tina studied her source. He was dressed in a trench coat and wearing a baseball cap, which was pulled down over his eyes.

"I've got some information for you."

"Okay, I'm listening."

"It seems the feds have been questioning some people at the Shimizu Corporation who told them there were three people who initially worked on the humanoid robot project: Carlos Medina, Ivan Kaminsky, and Allan Jackson. Apparently, Jackson died in a car accident years ago under possibly mysterious circumstances. All three were terminated by the company, the Shimizu Corporation, after working there for several years. They'd been told the project was over. However, Shimizu continued the project without them." Tina's source paused. "The feds just discovered one of them may have taken one of the robots and raised it. They think it's the Cuban or the Russian."

"Ivan is from Minsk," Tina said. "That's not in Russia." She rolled her eyes.

"Whatever. What do I care about those Commie countries?"

Tina had no desire to explain the geopolitics of the two countries to this Neanderthal; she lamented the American educational system.

"Anyhoo, the bigwigs in the DOD are very keen to get their hands on the robot so they can use it for war or whatever. I don't know." He was shuffling his right foot in a circular motion.

Shit! thought Tina.

He pushed a folder at her.

"What's this?" she asked, accepting the file.

"Background information," he explained and became very serious. "Remember, you didn't get this from me, and you don't know me." As Tina's source turned to depart, Tina noticed his intense blue eyes.

2

"Suzie, are you okay?" Assther asked. Suzie was standing next to the couch, motionless with a vacant stare.

"Suzie, are you okay?" Suzie repeated mechanically, her eyes unblinking.

"Suzie, what's wrong?" Assther asked, rising from the couch.

"Suzie, are you okay? Suzie, what's wrong?" Suzie repeated, and remained in the same position, expressionless.

"Suzie, please stop doing that!" Assther commanded sternly approaching the child.

"Suzie, are you okay? Suzie, what's wrong? Suzie, please stop doing that," Suzie continued.

Assther felt a surge of panic. *Jesus, what's going on with her?* she thought. *What do I do?* This must have been what Tina was describing to her. *How do I stop her from malfunctioning and keep her safe?* Assther felt a growing sense of urgency and desperation. She was aware that Suzie's condition would only worsen with time. Maybe Tina was right that her father had knowledge which could save Suzie. In order to fulfill her promise to Ezmy, Assther was prepared to explore any avenue available.

Grabbing her bag and keys, Assther said, "Let's go, Suzie."

"Suzie, are you okay? Suzie, what's wrong? Suzie, please stop doing that. Let's go, Suzie," the child repeated mechanically.

Assther gently grabbed Suzie by the hand and guided her out of the house.

While Assther drove, she turned up the volume of the radio to drown out Suzie's mantra. *Was this what Ezmy was going through? No wonder she didn't want to go home. No wonder she couldn't sleep at night. I'm so sorry, Ezmy, I just didn't understand. I didn't know what was going on.*

After pulling up to the house and parking the car, Assther said, "Let's go, Suzie."

"Let's go, Suzie. Let's go, Suzie. Let's go, Suzie," Suzie said.

Assther took the child out of the car and shut the door with her foot. Then she moved briskly up the walkway to the house and urgently knocked on the door.

Before long, Carlos opened the door and said, "Come in, mija. You and I have a lot to talk about and we don't have too much time."

Assther had the impression her father had been expecting them. He motioned her to sit on the couch and quickly closed the door. Carlos' eyes were narrowed, his body stiff. He walked to the window, shifted the curtains aside, and surveilled the street on both sides.

"Let's go, Suzie, Let's go, Suzie. Let's go, Suzie," Suzie continued with her chant.

Carlos watched Suzie for several minutes, then walked to his desk, opened it, and removed a U-shaped device. Slowly, he approached the child and cupped his hand behind her neck. Suddenly, Suzie slumped over on the couch, silent and motionless.

"What did you do to her?" Assther asked, springing to her feet.

"She's fine," Carlos said. "She's just in sleep mode." His tone was calm.

Assther stared hard at her father for a few minutes. "What do you mean sleep mode? How do you know how to do that?"

Carlos exhaled and turned to face her. "Please sit down, mija. We have to talk."

Wringing his hands, Carlos stood up and began pacing the wooden floor. Then, clenching and unclenching his hands, he said, "How do I begin?" He paused. "You see, we were kids back then, still in college. It started as a joke, of sorts."

"Papi, if you don't stop pacing and sit down, I'm going to have to medicate you. I'm a doctor now, I have the drugs to do it." She smiled faintly at him.

"Sorry, mija." Carlos sat down next to his daughter. "The three of us, Ivan, Allan and I were sitting at a bar, talking about robotics, AI, and cybernetics. We were joking that we could create a humanoid robot more sophisticated than had ever been created. Although it began as a joke, we thought 'Why not?' The prospect of creating something novel became very exciting. We would be pioneers remembered throughout history, like Einstein and Turing.

"We worked on the project in our spare time, after school, after work, and on weekends. Allan, the biomedical engineer, created a polymer exoskeleton which would encase the robot and would grow as the robot grew. Ivan and I created a neural network which integrated natural language processing, machine perception, and affective computing. For several years, we worked to refine the program and create a human developmental model." Carlos paused for a few minutes, closing his eyes and rubbing them with his fingers.

"After four years, we had a prototype. We provided Dr. Schmeck, who was one of our professors and our mentor, a demonstration of the finished model. He was impressed and immediately called one of his friends, Mr. Shimizu in Silicon Valley, who owned a biomedical engineering company. We presented the model to Mr. Shimizu, and he proposed we work for his company after graduation with the proviso that we bring our work with us."

Carlos glanced at Assther to gauge her reaction. Then he stood up and walked over to the counter and poured himself a glass of water. He held the glass in his hand. "The three of us were thrilled to continue to work together and refine our model, and so we accepted the offer. We should've suspected something when they pressured us to sign a non-disclosure agreement. But we were young and naïve." Carlos took a sip of water and set the glass down on the counter.

"After graduation, the three of us began working at Mr. Shimizu's state-of-the-art lab, perfecting our model and correcting any problems. Two years later, we presented the finished model to Mr. Shimizu. We called it Autonomous Self-Sustaining Humanoid Robot, ASSHeR for short. The robotinoid human was developed to mimic human development physically, cognitively and emotionally."

Quietly Assther listened to her father, looking at him intently and nodding.

"Is Suzie an ASSHer model?" she asked, glancing at the lifeless form.

"Yes." Carlos nodded. He felt exhausted, both physically and emotionally, and his face was etched with fatigue. *I still haven't told her the difficult part yet.* He sighed deeply.

Chapter 11

1

After their meeting, Tina's source returned to his car and started the engine. He had enjoyed his meetings with Tina and found her to be tenacious, resourceful, and intelligent. The information he'd been supplying Tina had been intended to produce a desired effect, and he knew that. What was going to occur in the near future had been decided by others much more powerful than either of them. He and Tina were both pawns in a complicated chess game, and they were expendable.

A long time ago, Tina's source had learned a valuable lesson when he attempted to assert his free will. Because he'd wanted to follow his desires, the course of his life had drastically changed. He'd been swiftly and severely punished. Now he knew better. As he approached his destination, he reduced his speed and parked the car. After he disembarked, Tina's source strolled the narrow path, which was hedged by neatly trimmed rose bushes, to the front door. As crickets chirped in the cool night air, he knocked twice and waited, gazing up at the dark moonless sky. Finally, the door swung open.

"Is it done?" asked the disembodied voice. "Come in."

"Yes, it's done," replied Tina's source.

"Good. It's almost time," Ivan said, and closed the door behind Allan.

2

Meanwhile, Tina sat in her car, trying to process what she had just been told. *What does all this mean?* She turned on the cabin light and began reading the file she had just been given. Quickly, she absorbed the information, flipping through the pages.

"SHIT!" Tina said. "It can't be!"

Tina tossed the file in the passenger seat and started the car. It was much worse than she could've ever imagined. While driving, in her mind's eye, Tina remembered little Jimmy; his small face, which dimpled when he smiled; the way he giggled when she chased him and said, "You can't catch me, Aunt Tina!"; the way his whole body wrapped around her when he hugged her (his arms, legs, and head) and he would whisper, "I love you, Aunt Tina." Oh, how she missed little Jimmy!

Then Tina remembered Eloise, and the shell of a person she'd become because she hadn't been able to bury her son. Now, only the ghost-like Eloise remained, unable to feel, always searching for her son, incapable of finding comfort.

It wasn't the normal grieving process, and Tina knew her sister hadn't been able to mourn properly. It distressed Tina to see her sister in such a state. Pushing any feelings of uncertainty aside, Tina was sure what must be done. Now, driving faster than the speed limit, Tina periodically glanced in the rearview mirror looking for flashing lights.

As Tina brought the car to an abrupt stop in front of a house, her overused brakes screeched in protest. Quickly shutting off the engine, she flung the door open with her foot and sprinted up the path to the front door–leaving the car door open.

3

Rising from the couch, Assther began preparing tea for them both. *He looks terrible*, she thought, looking over at her father. After handing him a cup, Assther sat next to him.

"Please continue, Papi," Assther said.

Carlos sighed deeply and began again. "About a month after we presented our ASSHeR model, Mr. Shimizu's assistant entered the lab and informed us the project was shutting down. Apparently, a government agency found some ethical concerns." Carlos paused for several minutes. "We were informed we had one week to finish what we were working on. And we were re-minded about our NDA. Naturally, we were all upset. We de-cided to meet to discuss the situation. Allan was very angry. He kept saying it wasn't fair, it was our property, and they couldn't take it from us. However, because of the fine print in the NDA, Allan's lawsuit against the company was unsuccessful."

Carlos' shoulders dropped and his gaze was downcast. "Then shortly afterwards we received the news that Allan had died in a car accident."

Assther remembered the day her father had left home abruptly after receiving a phone call. Looking at her father, she noticed his hands were trembling when her father took a sip of his tea. Assther placed her hand on his arm.

Listening to her father, Assther felt something nagging at her as though there was an image just out of focus. Her mind was struggling to process the information and help her solve the mystery. The pieces of the puzzle were about to coalesce and reveal a clear picture.

"Papi, did you name me Assther because of the project you'd been working on?" she asked, hoping that would bring the pic-ture into clearer focus.

Weakly, Carlos shook his head.

"What I had told you about being born through a surro-gate wasn't true," Carlos said, avoiding her gaze. Then he took a deep breath. "As you know, your mother had been very de-pressed after finding out about her infertility. She was despon-dent. I thought I was going to lose her," Carlos said. Assther waited for her father to continue.

"I took one of the ASSHer models, modified it, improved it, and that's —"

"Me!" Assther said, almost jumping off the couch. With a sudden clarity her entire life made sense. Like the old-fashioned movie projectors, Assther began to replay scenes in her mind, slowly at first then increasing in speed. She recalled memories from infancy to present time in explicit detail. Her parents bath-ing her as an infant; her mother's face as she sang her to sleep in her crib; her father reading her a bedtime story; baking with her mother, both laughing, elbow deep in flour; their vacation at the beach before her mother became ill; her mother's illness and death; her job; Ezmy and Suzie.

Finally, Assther understood what her mother meant in her letter when she described her as being exceptional and unique. Assther remembered her despair and anguish at discovering the secret at her mother's funeral. For years, Assther had speculated about her biological family; why they'd abandoned her and where they might be. After all these years of searching for the truth, the facts had finally been revealed to her.

Suddenly, Assther realized perhaps her emotions and relationships hadn't been real because she wasn't human. Assther's lashes beaded with tears, her face was contorted, and she turned to face her father.

Assther's recollections took less than a minute, and Carlos studied her closely.

"Mija, I don't want you to think that your experiences and memories are not real or authentic, because that's not true," Carlos said as if reading her thoughts. He trailed off, unable to continue, his voice choked with emotion. Fighting back tears, he attempted to gain control.

"You've changed the lives of everyone who's has been fortunate to know you and love you. You are compassionate and loving and exhibit more human qualities than most humans I have encountered. Please trust that what you've done and experienced is meaningful and genuine," Carlos said hoarsely. He reached out and grasped Assther's hand.

"I couldn't tell you all this information after your mother died. Unfortunately, now you're in danger. There's a reporter who's been working on a story, and she's been calling me."

"You mean Tina?" Assther asked, wiping her eyes with the back of her hand.

"How do you know Tina?" Carlos asked, his eyebrows lifting.

"I met her to talk with her about Suzie. Ezmy had talked to her about Suzie too, before she ...died."

Carlos nodded his head feebly.

"Tina told me about other children like Suzie who are mal-functioning." Assther paused. "Papi, why am I functioning normally?" It was a question that had been nagging at her.

Carlos raked his hand through his thick hair, sighed deeply, and replied, "Throughout your life, I've been adjusting your code, making sure it was updated and working properly. But when the company fired us and started mass producing the ASSHeR models, they didn't update the codes. So they malfunction or just stop working." Carlos' face was pale and haggard. "You have to understand, Assther. The circumstances were desperate." Carlos paused, his voice quivering. "I took an ASSHer model, modified it, and presented you to your mother. Assther, you saved her, and *we* became a family."

A large knot formed in Assther's throat as she listened to her father.

"If Tina has been investigating you, then others will be coming for you too. They'll come and take you away and make you do things ... maybe bad things that you don't want to do." His voice trailed off.

Assther was deep in thought for several minutes, considering the information. Then she looked at her father and said, "That sounds similar to what Tina said happened to her nephew, Jimmy." After a pause, she added, "I think I saw two men in suits watching me at Ezmy's funeral. Do you think they knew about Ezmy's will and Suzie?"

"I don't know," replied her father. "But it's possible."

"Papi, I don't see how people can make me do things I don't want to."

"They can do experiments on you, alter your coding and change you," Carlos replied, exhaling deeply.

"What do we do?" Assther asked with a heavy sigh. "You must have a plan."

"I promised your mother before she died that I would always protect you and keep you safe," Carlos said, his voice faltering. "That's what I'll do: protect you no matter what."

"Papi, I trust you," Assther said, looking intently into her father's eyes. "But I need you to promise to protect Suzie too."

"I promise, mija," Carlos said.

As they stood to embrace, both were weeping.

123

Chapter 12

1

"Mr. Medina, it's me, Tina Ho," Tina called out, pacing nervously outside the house. "We need to talk. It's important. Please let me in!"

Repeatedly, Tina rang the doorbell, peering into the windows for any signs of movement in the house. "Mr. Medina, it's me, Tina. We really need to talk. Please let me in!" She knocked again more insistently.

Soon, Tina began pounding her fists on the door. "Mr. Medina, please, they're coming for her. Please, open the door. We need to talk." There was desperation in her voice.

On the other side of the door, Carlos heard Tina's pleas.

Bang, bang, bang

"I know," Carlos whispered. "I'm way ahead of you."

Well aware of why Tina was at his doorstep, Carlos continued with his preparation. Months of meticulous planning had paid off just as he'd anticipated. The first part of Carlos' plan had been to pose as the lawyer and force Tina's editor to stop publishing her articles. Then he had insisted that Tina be reassigned. Afterward, Carlos had provided Tina with misleading information through her source, which would allow Carlos to complete the final phase of his plan. Although Assther nearly derailed his plan with her own investigation, everything was on track now. As intended, Tina would publish her story.

For many years, Carlos had known this moment would come. He and Hannah had discussed it many times. They both agreed that if and when the time arrived, he had to protect Assther at all costs. They'd formulated a plan, and the time had arrived to enact it.

Gingerly lifting Assther's limp form, Carlos transferred her to the living room and placed her in his favorite chair. He could still hear Tina pounding on his door.

"I'll keep my promise to both of you," Carlos said, staring at the wedding picture for several moments. Then he moved toward the record player, lifted the case, and turned on the machine. For the last time, silently with his eyes shut, Carlos listened to the music.

Then, turning to the bookcase, he pulled the corner of Einstein's *The Meaning of Relativity*. Suddenly, the bookshelf shifted to reveal a narrow passageway. Gently, Carlos cradled Assther in both arms and carried her through the damp and dark corridor. The odor of warm soil permeated the thin air.

They entered a second room, which was illuminated with rows of florescent lights suspended with fine filaments from the ceiling. A large metal workbench was arranged in the middle of the room, and a flickering computer was situated on a wooden desk. A cold chill escaped from the unfinished walls, which were ringed by metal shelves overflowing with tools. After resting Assther on the metal table, Carlos returned to the living room through the tunnel. He retrieved the wedding picture, picked up the immobilized Suzie, and went back to the frigid room. The bookcase slid shut behind him.

"We're going home," Carlos said, standing next to his daughter and stroking her hair. "Everything'll be fine now."

"It's great to see you, my friend," Ivan said, embracing Allan tightly. "I've missed you dearly."

Allan returned the embrace and said, "I missed you too, Ivan." After releasing his friend, Allan said, "It looks like life has been good to you."

"Sweets are my vice," Ivan said, chuckling and patting his wide girth.

Having removed his shoes at the foyer, Allan pinched his toes into the plush carpet and strolled around the room. He surveyed the high vaulted ceiling and the *objets d'art* from around the world that were displayed in glass cases. Allan lingered in front of several nude paintings decorating the wall.

"I see sweets are not your only vice," he said with a grin. Ivan reddened and moved to the large pewter samovar in the corner of the room.

"Allan, would you like some tea? The water is fresh."

Allan nodded mutely and strolled languidly to the couch. He noticed a crystal-cut candy dish on the glass coffee table. Slowly and deliberately, Allan removed the lid and retrieved a crimson piece of candy and placed it on his tongue. Then his lips puckered.

Ensconced in the supple leather couch, Allan noticed Dr. Schmeck seated at the dining room table swirling a spoon in a porcelain cup.

Dr. Schmeck cleared his throat and said, "Welcome back, Allan. It's nice to see you again." He hesitated for a minute and took a sip from his cup. "Even if it is for a short time."

"It's nice to see you, too," Allan said, attempting to maintain a neutral facial expression. He was surprised at his mastery for faked sincerity. Allan had had numerous opportunities to perfect the art.

After bringing Allan his tea, Ivan sat next to his friend on the couch. There was a prolonged silence as the two men exchanged glances and watched the older man.

"We've a received a directive to return home," Dr. Schmeck said, glancing at Ivan and Allan in turn. "Carlos is aware of the plan." Slowly resting his cup in its saucer, Dr. Schmeck rose and began pacing the length of the room.

"We should all be proud of the work we've done here." He stopped, turned, and considered his next words. "All those years ago, we were the first of our kind to be sent here. Although initially the plan had been to remain longer and gather more information, complications have made that impossible. However, our scientists will have more than enough data to analyze for years to come."

In silence, the two men waited for their former professor to continue.

"The ETA for transport will be in twenty-four hours," Dr. Schmeck said and returned to the dining room table and sat down. "After all these years, I'm sure you'll be glad to remove these coverings," he added with a faint smile.

2

A thick bank of clouds moved toward Tina. The air was crisp as the wind struck the towering oak tree nearby, causing the branches to creak. A group of ravens croaked in the distance.

Tina was distressed that she couldn't find either Carlos or Assther. And that she'd been unsuccessful in warning Carlos about the impending danger to Assther. Hoarse from screaming and both fists smarting from pounding the Medinas' front door, Tina squatted on the sidewalk to consider her next move. Both her energy and spirit were spent. Tina buried her head in the crook of her elbow and sobbed. She wept for Eloise and Jimmy, for Assther, and Suzie and Ezmy. But most of all, Tina wept for herself. She'd spent so much of her life painstakingly researching to uncover the truth, provide closure to Eloise, and prevent any other family from experiencing the same fate. But she'd failed.

A fury which had been germinating in Tina for years now consumed her. She wouldn't allow this injustice to continue. A cold shiver passed through her. Perhaps *they* had already taken Assther? Perhaps she was already too late. Tina had all the information she needed, and she knew what must be done.

Without warning, the earth began to vibrate under Tina's feet. Bracing for an earthquake, Tina scanned her surroundings for shelter. The vibration was accompanied by a rumbling, which intensified into a high-pitched whine. Tina felt as if a drill was piercing her ear drums, and she brought her hands up to muffle the sound. Becoming faint, she dangled her head between her knees and took several deep breaths.

Almost immediately, Tina glanced up and saw an intense shaft of light descending directly upon the Medina home. Despite shielding her eyes with her hands, the glow was still visible. Tina felt faint and her body and limbs were weak. She collapsed on the sidewalk.

In the future, when Tina would remember the events which had unfolded, she would recall that a split-second prior to losing consciousness, she'd seen a second flash of light strike another house. At that moment, Tina only saw darkness.

END

EIN HERZ FÜR AUTOREN A HEART FOR AUTHORS À L'ÉCOUTE DES AUTEURS MIA KAPΔIA ГIA ΣYГГPAΦ
UN CUARTA POR FÖRFATTARE UN CORAZÓN POR LOS AUTORES YAZARLARIMIZA GÖNÜL VERELIM SZIVÜ
JÖNS PER AUTORI ET HJERTE FOR FORFATTERE EEN HART VOOR SCHRIJVERS TEMOS OS AUTORE
SZÍVÜNKÉRT SERCE DLA AUTORÓW EIN HERZ FÜR AUTOREN A HEART FOR AUTHORS À L'ÉCOUTE
CORAÇÃO BCEЙ ДУШОЙ К ABTOPAM ETT HJÄRTA FOR FÖRFATTARE À LA ESCUCHA DE LOS AUTORE
AUTEURS MIA KAPΔIA ГIA ΣYГГPAΦEIΣ UN CUORE PER AUTORI ET HJERTE FOR FORFATTERE EEN HA
YAZARLARIMIZ GÖR VERE RE SZÍVÜNKÉRT SERCE DLA AUTORÓW EIN HERZ FÜR A
VOOR SCHRIJVERS TEMOS OS AUTORE CORAÇÃO BCEЙ ДУШОЙ К ABTOPAM ETT HJÄRTA FÖR F

The author

Rosa Golub is the pen name for Rahel Ruiz MD.
She was born in Ethiopia and escaped the revo-
lution with her family at the age of ten arriving
in Baltimore as a refugee. Her childhood dream
of becoming a doctor propelled her to work hard
academically and she graduated from Harvard
Medical School in 1996. She has been working as
Internist for the past 20 years and currently lives in
the San Francisco Bay Area with her husband and
two children.

The publisher

He who stops getting better stops being good.

This is the motto of novum publishing, and our focus
is on finding new manuscripts, publishing them and
offering long-term support to the authors.
Our publishing house was founded in 1997, and since
then it has become THE expert for new authors and
has won numerous awards.

**Our editorial team will peruse each manuscript
within a few weeks free of charge and without
obligation.**

You will find more information about
novum publishing and our books on the internet:

www.novumpublishing.com

CPSIA information can be obtained
at www.ICGtesting.com
Printed in the USA
BVHW072134230122
626572BV00001B/14